CRYPTID FORCE SIX: BAD VACATION

--BOOK 3--

LUCAS PEDERSON

SEVERED PRESS
HOBART TASMANIA

CRYPTID FORCE SIX: BEAT THE DEVIL

ONE

"Gah," Benny said. "The hell is *that*?"

Cujo rolled his eyes and aimed his gun at the small, scampering menace. Not the M16, but an M4 now. The AC-900 he reserved for larger targets. Still, he missed his 16. Old habits, he kept telling himself.

Old habits...

"What we're here for," Cujo said. The answer to Benny's question hung in the dry air of a southern Arizona afternoon like a bad joke.

What they found, however, was not why they were sent into the scorching badlands.

A bead of sweat trickled down the side of Cujo's sunburned face. He swallowed and winced at the dry click his throat made. His M4 remained trained on the thing digging into the side of a cow. It tossed red ribbons of meat in every direction. Wasting more than it ate.

"Well," Benny said. "That doesn't exactly look like a Mogollon Monster, man."

"Maybe it is," Cujo said, keeping his aim true on the creature.

"Uh, Dr. Reece said Mogollons are seven feet tall and hairy." Benny pointed at the cow-eating creature. "That's the size of a turkey, my dude."

Cujo grunted. "Maybe Reece was wrong."

"She's the expert, man."

"Sometimes experts get things wrong," Cujo said.

"Sometimes experts—did you hit your head back there somewhere?"

"Nope." The creature popped its head out of the carcass but ducked back inside before Cujo could squeeze off a round. He sighed, lowered the M4, and wiped sweat from his face.

"Doc has been right about a lot of—"

Cujo snorted. "I'm just fuckin' with ya, kid."

Benny blinked, frowned, and punched Cujo's shoulder. "Don't do that shit, man. Bad enough half the country has gone fruit-batty, I can't lose you too."

"Aww," Cujo said and flashed a smile at Benny.

Benny hit him in the shoulder again. A bit harder this time. He frowned. "I liked you better before CF6. I miss that boring old man."

"CF6?"

Benny sighed. "Cryptid Force Six. I mean, what—"

The creature pounced from the cow onto Benny, instantly clawing at his face and shoulders.

Cujo drew his knife and buried the blade into the creature's small head. He peeled the thing off Benny who jumped away, trembling. A few cuts littered his wide-eyed face. Cujo pulled a plastic bag free from his belt and dropped the creature in it. Something similar in shape to a medium-sized dog, a cocker spaniel perhaps, though its skin appeared reptilian. Dry and scaly.

He sealed the bag. Reece would figure it out.

They were there to stop a rampaging Mogollon. Something like a Bigfoot, Reece told him, only a bit shorter. The thing was supposed to be covered in hair or fur too. Been spotted killing cattle and a couple of people. The video evidence was convincing enough to pique Reece and Ross's interests. Not enough to send out the entire team, though. It was more of a recon mission in Cujo's eyes. Nothing too serious.

Cujo pressed his throat mic and said, "Bagged a strange critter. Not the Mogollon."

A few seconds later, Reece said, "Description of the creature you bagged?"

He sighed, held it up and squinted at the dead creature through the clear plastic bag. "Dog-like in shape, but its skin is scaly. Long fangs—"

"Chupacabra," Reece said. "They're everywhere in that region."

"So...you want us to toss the corpse?" Benny asked.

"No. Bring it in. I need a new specimen to study."

Cujo grunted. "Like I need a vacation."

Benny clapped Cujo on the back. "Right? Fuck sake, we've been on a three year stretch already."

Reece didn't say anything for a few minutes, giving Cujo and Benny enough time to drag the mutilated cow into the brush for scavengers to devour.

"Head north," Reece said. "Mogollons hide around the stone structures and caves."

Benny pulled up a map on his tablet. They were about a mile from any stone structures judging by the nearest geography. Though she admitted before they departed, she wasn't exactly sure where the stone structures were. Just an educated guess and might not be on the map.

Cujo sighed and pressed the throat mic. "We'll check out the site a mile north of us, but if we don't find anything, tell Ross we're coming home."

"Ten-four," Reece said.

Cujo looked at Benny and Benny looked at him.

"Ready to find a knockoff Bigfoot?"

Benny grinned. "Thought you'd never ask."

***

The place they drove to wasn't on the map. It just existed. Maybe the indigenous people knew about it. Regardless, someone forgot to publicize it like the spots near the Grand Canyon.

Strange, Cujo thought. *It's quite beautiful.*

Red stone hills which appeared to be sanded into unique, abstract sculptures by gods unknown and out of time, stretched for what appeared to be miles. Like most of the landscape in Arizona, except this place has plants. Cactus, weeds, bushes, and flowers of all types flourished. Contrasted against the rusty-red of the stone and dirt, it was indeed beautiful. A vista worth a million pictures. Memories kept.

Cujo never liked the tropical regions or the desert regions. Extreme heat, both wet and dry, wasn't something he considered fun. Despite this, however, he found it all to have its certain charms. Nature was as beautiful as it was mysterious.

"I don't get it," Benny said and took a swig from his canteen.

Cujo blinked and retreated from his thoughts. "Don't get what?"

"This is like a rocky desert, man. How are all these plants living?"

Cujo shrugged, gaze scanning the landscape. Beauty be damned, they were there to hunt down a killer cryptid. "Maybe there's a water source nearby."

Benny grunted. "Here? Dude, this place is a fucking—"

A large rock about the size of Cujo's head thumped to the ground inches from Benny's boots, kicking up a plume of rust-colored dust.

Benny stumbled away, coughing and waving his hand to clear the dust while Cujo remained where he was and lifted his M4.

"Fuckin' hell," Benny said and waved more of the red dust away. "What was that?"

"Rock," Cujo said, focusing on a mound a lighter shade of red about twenty yards directly in front of them. He hadn't noticed it before.

"A rock? Did that thing just seriously throw a rock at me?"

"Shh," Cujo said. "Our twelve. Look for a lighter shade of red than the stones."

Benny fell silent for a bit, then grunted. "See it." Another pause. "Target in the crosshairs, Boss."

Cujo waited a few seconds, then, "Drop it."

Benny's M107 clacked, but the mound didn't drop. Instead, a white spot appeared at the center.

"Um," Benny said, "I think I just killed a rock."

Heart stuttering, Cujo swung his M4 to the left—

The roar was enough to make Cujo stumble back a step or two. Not due to lack of balance, but the sheer shock and terror it induced.

He spun and something large smacked the carbine out of his hands. He shuffled backward, drew his pistol and fired three shots into the creature's orange broad chest. None of which seemed to phase the thing. Hell, it didn't even flinch.

Cujo sidestepped, aimed the pistol at the creature's face but it was too quick and shoved him so hard he went flying. He hit the dirt hard, rolled and came to a rest against one of the smaller stone structures. He tried to stand and collapsed, back screaming in agony. He rolled onto his right side and stared at two large feet. The dark skin was cracked and heavily calloused. The nails were all long and ragged.

"Ah, shit," Benny said. "I got it, Boss."

Cujo couldn't move. His back hurt too damn much and the thing was right on top of him. If he tried anything he'd be pounded into a hamburger before he even got a shot off.

Instead, he waited for Benny.

And waited…

"You gonna shoot it or jerk off?" Cujo shouted through the pain clutching his back.

The large feet shifted, stirring up red dust. The beast roared.

Heart stammering, Cujo knew this was it. Soon it'd slam its heavy fists down onto his back, breaking it. Then it would bash his head in with a rock or—

It whined, snorted, and the large feet stumbled away. Blood dripped onto its wriggling toes. Then it dropped hard to the ground in an explosion of red dust.

Cujo rolled away, back screaming, trying to breathe through all the dust. He coughed, every inhale triggering another and another and—

Strong arms heaved him upward and dragged him out of the red cloud.

"Gotcha, Boss," Benny said, leaning Cujo against one of the smaller stone structures.

Cujo, still coughing, though finally taking in clean air, shifted away from the structure. He about fell onto his side before Benny caught him and sat him upright again. In doing so it made Cujo's back roar in agony, so he shifted again and about fell face first into dirt.

Benny, once more sitting him upright, "What's your deal, man?"

Cujo, finally catching his breath, face crimped with pain, managed, "Back."

"Oh," Benny said and helped Cujo lay on his side. A couple of seconds later, he was on the throat mic talking to Reece. "Need emergency transport." He read out the coordinates. "Something with Cujo's back. Yep. Okay."

Benny hunkered down beside Cujo. "Help is on the way, Boss."

Cujo nodded and winced. His gaze drifted to the large orange mound a few feet away. A pool of blood darkened the dirt crimson around the beast's head.

Christ, he thought. *I really need a vacation.*

TWO

It took longer than Cujo expected with all the aches and pains, but he eventually made his way from his quarters to the mess hall. Well, Ross called it a cafeteria, but whatever.

Most of his team were already there chowing down like gluttons. His old drill sergeant would've overturned tables and kicked some ass seeing them in such lax positions. Benny scrolling on his phone. Luna reading a book while nursing what appeared to be a cherry pie. Maze tapping away on a tablet for God knew what reasons. There was no discipline. They might as well be civilians now. In a way, they pretty much were.

Ellen sat alone in the far corner, head lowered. Her food appeared untouched.

The aroma of grilled meat drew him deeper into the cafeteria.

"Well, holy shit," Benny said. "Ya sure you're healed up enough to walk, Boss?"

This caught everyone's attention and of course they all stared at him. He was getting used to it, but such intense attention took him aback at times. Cujo waved them away and walked to the serving line.

Ham, grilled chicken breasts, beef brisket, mashed potatoes, steamed broccoli, mac and cheese...

Same dinner every day. Breakfast was scrambled eggs, bacon, and pancakes. Lunch...your choice of chicken noodle or tomato soup and ham or turkey sandwiches.

All the same. Day in and day out. He liked the food. Kirby Ross hired the best chefs and staff, but it all just became so...redundant. Living the same life over and over. Eating the same foods. Talking to the same people. He loved his team like family, but a little space would be nice. Not to mention there were more cryptids than he ever thought possible, not including variations and Government splices. The list was endless.

Cujo grabbed his chow and sat down at a table away from the rest of the team.

"You okay, Pops?" Maze called from across the cafeteria.

He waved a dismissive hand at her and went about stuffing his face.

His back was still sore, though tolerable. Ross's doctors determined that Cujo slipped a couple of discs in his back, which brought on the agony. The result accumulated to being over sixty years old, a lifetime in the military, and being thrown into a stone structure by a Bigfoot wannabe. With the discs back in place, he hoped the pain would go away soon.

The brisket was perfectly smoked, like always. Cujo mixed it with his mashed potatoes. Changing it up a bit.

He had lived most of his life through routine and now…well…he was just toodamn tired.

Luna plopped down across from him, book in hand. "Hey. How's the back?"

Cujo grunted, shoveled a couple of bites into his mouth, and didn't reply.

A frown creased her otherwise cool, placid features. "What's wrong?"

Cujo ate his dinner.

"Something's wrong," Luna said.

"There is?" Maze said and took a chair on Cujo's right.. She gave Cujo a nudge. "What's wrong, Ol'Hoss?"

"If it's because you're old," Benny said, sitting down on Cujo's left, "I call bullshit."

"He's tired," Ellen said from the aisle. She didn't move any closer and her gaze kept darting to Maze.

Trouble between them, Cujo thought.. Best not to get into romantic relationships with people you work with daily…your proverbial family. Love was love. Definitely. Absolutely. But a romantic relationship in a working environment came with a price, sometimes. He saw it plenty of times throughout the years. They need to—

A shrill alarm blared, cutting through the tension like a butcher's knife.

They all glanced at each other.

Cujo took a bite of brisket and mashed potatoes, swallowed and said, "Sounds like a perimeter breach alarm."

They hustled out of the cafeteria.

Cujo grunted, finished the food on his tray, placed the tray with the rest of the dirty ones, and followed his team.

It was probably just a drill anyway.

THREE

The creature tore through the electrified wired outer perimeter and bounded across the eighty-yard space between outer and inner perimeters. Eighty yards which was supposed to be lined with mines, beartraps and motion sensor turrets. Yet somehow the creature avoided them all.

"Why aren't the turrets firing?" Cujo said.

They stood in the Monitor Room. A twelve foot by twelve-foot room that smelled a little like cottage cheese and onions. A room reserved for four guards to keep an eye out for any strange activity around the compound.

Until now, their jobs had been pretty damned uneventful.

"Is it moving too fast?" Maze said.

"The sensors are acute," Kirby Ross said and crossed his arms over his narrow chest. "Even the slightest movement should trigger them."

"You should see how many birds and squirrels those things blast through," Jeff, one of the younger guards assigned to the Monitor Room said. "It's—"

"Not relevant, Jeffery," the eldest guard, Nick, said. Cujo assumed Nick's age to be early to mid-sixties. About the same age as Cujo, anyway.

The younger man nodded and lowered his head, doing everything he could to avoid eye contact with everyone. The boy was definitely a rookie. Cujo had seen his fair share of boys like him through the years. Hell, he used to be one too, a million years ago it seemed.

"Twenty yards to the inner perimeter," Nick said. "Fifteen yards."

"What the hell is it?" Benny asked.

"Reece?" Cujo said.

But Amanda Reece only shook her head. "Moves too fast. I can't get a good visual of it."

"I can send a recorded clip to you," Nick said. "Maybe you can slow it down."

"Yes," she said. "Please. And hurry."

The inner perimeter was made up of fifty-foot reinforced steel walls, motion activated turrets, and heat signature turrets. The top of the wall was festooned with feet of titanium razor wire.

Kirby Ross's compound was built to withstand a small invasion. Yet, this lone creature was slipping by all the defenses.

Reece worked on the video Nick sent her. Slowing it down and checking out different angles.

Cujo sighed and walked toward the door.

"Where ya going, Boss?"

"Gearing up," Cujo said. "If it gets through the inner perimeter, we're the last line of defense."

"Your back, Pops," Maze said. "You'll cripple yourself."

Cujo grunted and left the room.

She was right, of course, his back wasn't healed enough to fight a cryptid, let alone one as fast as this one. Still, what the hell was he supposed to do? Just sit in that cramped room watching the creature get closer and closer to killing someone? No. He'd be damned if he let that happen.

He was in the locker room getting geared up (and wincing at every sudden movement) when Maze and Benny slammed open the door and came storming in.

Cujo slipped into his Kevlar vest and tried his best not to cry in pain.

"You're staying inside," Maze said.

Cujo snorted, buckling the gun belt and holsters around over his hips. "Not a chance."

"No," Benny said. "Really, man. Sit this one out. Rest that back."

He spun on them. "I'm fine. Get geared up. I don't think we have much—"

"Reece thinks it's a Van Meter Monster," Maze said.

Cujo opened his mouth, closed it, and frowned.

"Fast bastard," Benny said. "Eight-foot wingspan. Like a goddamn pterodactyl, man."

"Only it has some kind of horn on its forehead," Maze said. "It reflects light to confuse and stun its prey."

Cujo blinked. "So, it's just going to fly over the inner perimeter wall." He hurried about as best he could to get the rest of his gear on.

"Doesn't work like that." Reece stepped around Maze and held up the tablet.

"Christ," Cujo said. "Is there no privacy in this world anymore? Why don't you all invite half of Des Moines in here while you're at it."

"Van Meter Monster," Reece said, as if Cujo hadn't spoken at all, "is only one of three real cryptids in Iowa and the most abundant."

"Never heard of it," Cujo said, still working into the rest of his gear.

"Gray, eight-foot wingspan, lightning quick. Half man, half animal with bat-like wings. Remind you of anything?"

"Jersey Devil," Cujo said.

"Yes," Reece said. "The Van Meter Monster is slightly different, though. It is much faster and has a reflective horn to blind its victims."

"So, why is it here?" Cujo asked. "Why does it seem to have a purpose?"

"That," Reece said and tapped on her tablet, "is unknown. All I know from research is this cryptid is extremely fast and cunning."

"That means," Maze said and leaned against the locker next to Cujo, "you need to sit this one out, Pops."

He snorted. "Not a chance in Hell." He slammed his locker door and pushed by them.

"I have read the doctor reports," Reece said.

Cujo stopped. Those bastards weren't supposed to—

"There's more to your diagnosis than a couple of slipped discs."

He lowered his head, though didn't turn around.

"Wait, what?" Benny said.

"Do you want to tell them, or should I?" Reece said.

Jaw clenched, Cujo turned to Reece, Maze and Benny. The latter two appeared to be on the verge of tears. Fully concerned. Something he was trying to avoid by keeping things quiet. Until now…

"Look," Cujo said, "I didn't want you all to worry."

"What the fuck is going on?" Maze spouted.

Cujo sighed, lowered his head and tried to think of a good way to say what needed to be said. It didn't take him long.

"I have cancer."

Both Maze and Benny blinked. They opened their mouths then closed them.

Cujo manifested a smile. "Only stage two. Not that serious."

"Not that—Dude, were you really trying to keep it from us?" Benny appeared genuinely hurt.

"Yep," Cujo said. "Better things to worry about than me."

"The fuck you say?" Benny nearly shouted. "You're our goddamn leader. We're…we're *family*, man!"

"I know that," Cujo said. "And like I said, it's only stage two."

Maze sighed. "I don't care if it's stage one, Pops. You should've told us."

"And what fucking good would that have done?" He slammed an open locker door. "Huh? What good would it have done? Like now. What good is it doing? While we stand here talking about it a monster is trying get into the compound."

He turned and stormed out of the locker room.

"Hey," Wade said, catching Cujo a few feet away from the locker room door. "Everything okay? Sounded like—"

Cujo cocked a thumb over his shoulder. "They'll brief you. Get geared up. We have an immediate threat to take care of."

He hurried toward the armory before Wade could say anything more.

Yes, cancer sucked. The very word brought with it its own kind of horror. And it sucked he had it. But there was a job to be done and no time to waste. Other than a sore back, though, he felt fine. He was just lucky Kirby Ross had the best in medical technology, and beyond. The contraption they used on him slipped the discs back in without any issues. Crackle, pop, and it was done in less than ten minutes. The damn thing also gave him a nice massage. Then they injected him with something that was supposed to work slower, but eventually completely heal his back. Nanotech, one doctor called it. The only catch was he needed to rest for a couple of weeks otherwise the damage wouldn't get repaired correctly. As for the cancer, he refused to let them inject him with an experimental cure. If he died, he wanted it because of something he couldn't control. His choice.

Cujo used his keycard to open the armory doors and rushed to the small section of wall where his weapons waited. He holstered his pistol, grabbed the M4, and paused. After a second or two, he took the AC-900 down and slung it over his shoulder.

"You stay behind the others," a smooth voice spoke from behind Cujo.

"Damn," Cujo said. "You're a sneaky bastard, Ross."

"I'm serious, Arron. We can't afford to lose you or have you injured further before you completely heal."

"Yeah, well, if I go down…I'm going down fighting." He turned and faced Ross. "End of discussion."

But Kirby Ross slowly shook his head. He crossed his arms over his narrow chest. His glasses slid down his nose a bit. "No. It's not the end of the discussion. I'm your boss and I'm telling you to stand back and let the others handle the threat. You'll be backup."

"My boss?" Cujo moved closer to Ross, glaring. "We're not mercenaries."

To his credit, Ross didn't back down, and Cujo admired that. "No. You are not mercenaries, but you are under my payroll and if you wish to remain here, please follow orders."

Cujo blinked. This was a first. No one besides higher-ranking officers had told him what to do in the past. Now…he was being ordered by a billionaire.

The other five of the team burst in, all geared up and grabbing their weapons.

Cujo sighed. He hated to back down, but… "Fine. I'll play backup."

Ross nodded. "Good. See that you do." He turned and walked out of the armory.

Their entire time in the compound, Ross had never been so stern with any of them. Until now.

Again, Cujo kind of admired that. Like a disgruntled officer who never really saw much battle before, but knew what he was talking about for the good of the platoon.

"I'll let ya get a shot or two in, Pops," Maze said and clapped him gently on the back. "No worries, Ol' Feller." She rushed out of the armory before he could tell her off.

He started to follow her when Benny darted in front of him. "Crippled man walkin'! We got a crippled man walkin' here!" His Southern accent was nothing short of hideous.

Cujo punched the kid's shoulder. "Keep it up and you'll be the crippled man, ass-hat."

"Ouch," Benny said. "Careful everyone, he's a hostile cripple!"

Luna chuckled and gave Cujo a gentle pat on the shoulder before hurrying out of the armory.

Benny fell back to walk beside Cujo. "You sure about this, Boss?"

Cujo didn't look at the man as they stepped out of the armory. "Yep."

"Okay. But if you break a hip out there, I'm strapping you to a chair next time."

Cujo shot him a glare. "You—"

"Toodles." Benny sprinted away, laughing.

Cujo sighed, clenched his jaw, and followed his team outside.

FOUR

"It stopped at the inner perimeter," Reece said through Cujo's earbud. "Appears to be calculating its next move. Incredible specimen, too."

Benny pressed his throat-mic. "Want us to leave you two alone for a bit?"

"Shut up, Benny," Reece spouted.. She waited a few beats and said, "It's located in the fourth quadrant of the compound. Northern point."

The team hurried in that direction, Cujo in tow. He kept his pace steady, back twinging in pain every now and then, and realized they were right. He wouldn't be worth a damn in the lead until his back healed. In fact, he'd probably get someone killed.

Sometimes getting old was bullshit.

They stopped near the north gate. Which wasn't a gate at all, but a staircase, and an elevator leading to the top of the wall.

Maze nodded at the elevator. "High ground. If that fucker is gonna climb the wall, we can have the advantage."

"What if it flies?" Benny said. "Reece said it has wings."

"Then we'll shoot it when it's flying. C'mon." Maze jogged toward the elevator, but no one followed her. When she noticed, she stopped and faced the team. "Y'all coming?"

Benny glanced back at Cujo. Luna, Ellen and Wade followed suit.

The sun was already dipping toward the horizon. The dogdays of August. Summer's final hoorah. It would be dusk soon. Harder to see and calculate distances. Still, Cujo waited for Maze. She was the commanding officer right now. A position she wanted from the beginning yet conceded to Cujo later on. They made quite the commanding duo, Cujo admitted, if they could find themselves on the same page, at least.

Cujo looked at Maze. "Split up. Three on top, three on the ground."

Maze opened her mouth, about to say something, then closed it and nodded. She pointed at Ellen. "El and Benny, come with me."

Benny on top. Good call. A sniper as good as him could pick off a moving target if he had to and high ground was always best. Did it a few times both in their platoon and on the Cryptid Force Six. The kid was a master marksman if ever there was one.

Cujo had the tanks of the team on the ground. Luna and Wade

Luna with her M203 grenade launcher attached to an M16A3 and a M32A1. Though she only brought the M203 and M16A3 combo now. He wished she had the M32A1. That beast of a rotary grenade launcher would come in handy.

He watched half of their team ascend to the top of the fifty-foot wall and turned to Luna and Wade. "Back up fifty yards. Find a good hiding place."

"Ambush?" Luna said.

"Yup. If we catch it off guard, maybe we have a chance. It's too fast otherwise."

"What if it gets by us?" Wade said.

Cujo shrugged. "Then hopefully Ross has a backup plan."

They each found their hiding places about fifty yards from the wall. Wade crouched behind a Jeep. Luna found a shallow alcove of the main facility. Cujo kneeled ten yards farther back, partially hidden behind a sign directing supply trucks to go to the West Bay.

"We have a visual," Maze spoke through the earbud. "It's just standing there at the bottom."

"I have a bead on it," Benny said. "This'll be done in less than—oh, *shit!*"

Cujo's heart stuttered. He pressed the throat mic. "Maze? Benny? Ellen? Come back!"

Nothing but static.

"Maz—"

"It's comin' your way, Pops," Maze shouted. "We're on our way down!"

Cujo's gaze snapped to the bruised sky. He didn't see anything.

At first...

A silvery wisp caught the attention of his peripheral vision. He glanced to the left just in time to watch the creature swoop down and land little more than ten yards away. Its skin was a light gray. Its head was long like a horse and filled with pointy teeth. A small, shiny horn protruded from the thing's forehead which sent out near blinding flashes every time it moved its head.

The Van Meter Monster moved on the talons of its wings and rear legs shaped like a lion's hind legs though ending in bird-like claws. The body itself reminded Cujo of a bat. The creature stood at least seven feet and that was on all fours.

Cujo's attention shifted from the monster to Luna, who was fully exposed. They hadn't expected it to land this far in. She was about twenty feet behind the creature. If it turned around...

Luna aimed her M203 at the thing and nodded at Cujo, signaling for him to move. He was well within the grenade blast radius.

Moving as slow as possible, trying not to make a sound while his back screamed at him to stop with the goddamn twisting and shifting and the whole mobile thing. He gritted his teeth against the pain and fell back anyway.

The heel of his boot scuffed a bit of gravel and he stopped.

A low hiss slithered through the air.

Heart hammering, Cujo stared at what he could see of the creature from under the sign. It didn't move. The hissing stopped.

Cujo continued backing away until he was about twenty feet away. He kneeled and switched from the M4 to the AC-900. It was a huge cryptid. Nothing like the giant yetis a couple of years ago up north. Still, the AC-900 fired twenty rounds per second. The fastest fire rate he ever encountered. The Van Meter Monster was extremely fast after all.

"We see ya, Pops," Maze spouted in his ear. "We're about ten feet to ground level."

Cujo cringed, hoping the creature didn't hear her voice through the earbud.

It still didn't move.

Come on, Luna, he thought. *Blast it.*

But she never did. Instead, the monster slowly rounded the sign and stared directly at Cujo with narrow, dark eyes.

He drew in a breath, and pointed his gun at the creature.

"My launcher is jammed," Luna said in his ear. "Hold on, Cujo."

"We're en route," Maze said.

"Coming," Wade said.

Meanwhile, the monster lowered its head like the predator it was. A deep growl rumbled the air. It began to circle Cujo. Those dark eyes. He'd never seen such emptiness before, even in the Jersey Devils.

It faked to the right, swerved to the left and darted straight at him.

Cujo squeezed the trigger of his supped-up assault rifle.

It only took three seconds.

Three seconds. Sixty rounds.

Then it was on top of him.

His back no longer screamed but howled in agony.

In his ear, the team shouted things he couldn't understand while he struggled with the monster trying to rip him apart. He drew his pistol and fired six rounds into the creature's side. After the sixth, it shrieked and hopped off him.

Agony pulsed through him. He rolled onto his side, ready to put another round into the monster when his team opened fire.

His arm dropped and all the strength leaked out of him.

Somewhere in all the gray fog, Benny said, "We need to get him to medical."

FIVE

Warmth slipped over his face.

His eyes opened to slits against all the brightness of the outside world.

He tried to move, but the best he could do was lift an arm before it plopped back down onto the bed he lay in.

A bed?

Not his bed, though. The mattress felt too…stiff. Unused. Too new. So, where was he? Not his quarters, but…

"Can you hear me, Captain Wright?"

Cujo groaned and closed his eyes. The voice was too loud.

"You're in the medical ward," the voice said, though they might as well have been shouting. "Can you feel your toes, Captain Wright?"

What a stupid question. Of course he could feel his…

But he couldn't. Did someone cut off his feet?

He tried to tell the nurse or doctor no, but his voice seemed to be out of order.

Cujo shook his head, opening his eyes a little at a time. His vision cleared, giving way to a young man he hadn't been introduced to yet. Not one of Ross's doctors. An aide, maybe? The man appeared tall, though not scrawny. Broad in the chest and shoulders. Short, dark hair and deep brown gaze to his eyes. Deep, but Cujo noted a bit of steel in them too. Strength.

The man was a soldier. Perhaps a well-seasoned one, despite his younger age, which Cujo assumed to be late twenties to early thirties. But if a soldier, then why…

The man smiled. "I'm a veteran, if you're wondering. Marine. Semper fi. Oorah. Connor Hayes is my name."

Cujo opened his mouth but, once again, his voice failed him.

"Relax, Captain. I'm also a Registered Nurse. Brought onto the medical team a couple of days ago." He sighed, pulled a stool on rollers over and sat. "So, you can't feel your toes?"

Cujo shook his head. He swallowed and his throat made a dry click. He pointed at his throat.

Connor nodded, picked up a mug and brought the straw to Cujo's lips. It took a second or two because his mouth was too dry to provide a seal around the straw, but he eventually got it. A couple of sips. One to wet his mouth, the other to revive his throat. He coughed up a wad of phlegm. Connor provided a bowl for him to spit into.

"Why…can't I move…my legs?" For the first time since waking up, terror filled Cujo.

"The Van Meter Monster tousled you enough to slip those discs back out, and an extra one. They're all in place now, but there's more damage than before. I'm afraid it's a day-to-day situation now."

Cujo's heart stuttered. "Day-to-day situation? For what?"

"I'm going to give it to you straight, Captain." Connor's brown gaze never left Cujo. "There's a possibility you won't gain full use of your legs after this latest attack."

Cujo blinked. "What?" He took another drink, cleared his throat and frowned at Connor. "I was walking just fine before."

"The new disc that slipped did it," Connor said. "Dr. Rollings says the nanotech he injected, after he got you all readjusted, should heal you. But he also said you should be able to feel your toes after you wake up."

Cujo looked away. "Where is he?"

"Who?"

Cujo snapped a glare at Connor. "Dr. Rollings. Get the fuckin' doctor here. Now."

Connor opened his mouth and closed it again. He sighed, nodded, and walked away from Cujo's bed.

He hadn't meant to be so harsh, but when you wake up and find out you might not be able to walk, even though the doctor thought he would be able to, shit got real. Cujo, grunting, tried with all his strength to wiggle his toes. Nothing. He tried lifting his legs off the bed and only the right one rose about six inches. At least he could do that much.

It didn't take Dr. Rollings long to get to the med-bay with Connor following quickly behind. The man was short, bald, with a rosy, jolly face. A face with a white beard, which might be confused for Santa Claus.

"Connor says you wish to see me, Captain?"

"Yeah. What's all this about me not walking?"

Rollings nodded. "Ah, okay. Yes, it is a possibility, but an exceptionally low one. And with nanotech working on your spine as we speak, you'll still be able to walk, just not as well as you once did. Of course, you could also be completely healed in a month too."

Cujo lifted an eyebrow. "So, it's fifty-fifty?"

"As I see it, yes. If you can't wiggle your toes, can you lift either of your legs?"

"Yeah. Both of them. Not very high, though."

Rollings chuckled. "Well, that still means your legs are working. Give it a few days and we'll see how much progress we make."

"What if there isn't any?"

"Well," Rollings said and patted Cujo's shoulder. "Then we reassess everything, don't we?"

Cujo nodded. "Guess so. Thanks, Doc."

Rollings waved a dismissive hand. "No thanks necessary. I'll leave you in the care of Connor, here. He's the top of his class and knows more than I do sometimes."

Connor smiled, shaking his head. "Doubt it. But thank you, Dr. Rollings."

Again, Rollings waved a dismissive hand. "I'll check back in a couple of days. Just don't kill him during that time."

Connor smiled and said, "We'll see how onery he gets."

Rollings patted Connor on the back and hurried away. Cujo wondered what the man did when he wasn't being jolly and injecting people with nanotech? Did he work on jigsaw puzzles? The boat in a glass bottle thing? Did he paint or write? Hell, for all Cujo knew the man spent his off time at a gun range.

"Okay," Connor said and reclaimed the rolling stool beside Cujo's bed. "You trust me now?"

"Nope."

Connor snorted. "I wouldn't either. But do you trust me enough to take your vitals? Blood pressure, temperature, pulse? Shit like that?"

Cujo shrugged. "Sure. Just don't kill me like Doc said."

"Well," Connor said and flashed a grin. "We'll see what happens."

For some reason this struck Cujo as hilarious and he laughed through the time it took for Connor to take his blood pressure. By the time the kid was taking his temperature, the giggles subsided, thank God. He felt an idiot for laughing so much. Then again, he had gone through some traumatic shit there for a moment.

Either way, you'll still be able to walk, he told himself. *Suck it up and make it work.*

He worried about the team, though. Maze would make a fine leader, but she was still too inexperienced. There was no doubt in his mind she'd take the bull by the horns and succeed as time went on, though. Still, they were all his family and he didn't want to leave them just yet…if ever.

"Looking good," Connor said, and winked. "Except for your face."

Cujo rolled his eyes and flashed Connor his middle finger.

They laughed a bit and Connor said he'd be back to check on Cujo soon. The aides would be rolling through with a food cart in the next hour too.

About a half hour passed when he realized he was the only one in the med-bay. A reminder of how secluded they really were. As far as Cujo knew, there were only four teams in Kirby Ross's compound. The

Cryptid Force Six, Rescue, Clean Up Crew, and Intel. Of course, none of them really did much unless Cujo's team was on a mission. He supposed Rescuemight be out and about saving folks. A group of surly, raunchy dudes you wouldn't think cared about anyone but themselves and you'd be wrong. Their leader, Helen, was one of the nicest people Cujo had ever met.

Cujo took another few drinks of water and laid there while Connor took his vitals and sleep washed over him.

SIX

Two weeks later, Cujo was able to stand and walk on his own. Wobbly, but at least he was walking. A good sign, Dr, Rollings told him.

Maze, Benny and Luna helped with his physical training. All three of them would push him a tiny bit each day. Every now and then Wade and Ellen would pop in with pizza or beer, even though Dr. Rollings said no alcohol.

Another couple of weeks passed. The team went on a mission to investigate a possible Bigfoot lair north of Minnesota and the Lake of the Woods region without him. He had Reece report to him every fifteen minutes and couldn't stop pacing until they discovered the lair was only an old bear den.

"Figures," Benny said over the speakers in the med-bay. "Without Cujo none of the cryptids wanna play with us now. Way to go, Old Man."

"Yeah, thanks, Pops," Maze said.

"I wonder if he's even listening," Luna asked.

"Oh," Benny said. "He's listening, that crafty bastard."

Cujo sat on his bed and smiled. The kid knew him too well.

"That's kind of creepy," Ellen said.

"Says the woman who loves horror movies," Maze said.

"Hush, you."

"Cryptid Force, uh…five, over and out," Benny said.

The speakers fell silent and Cujo stood from the bed. His legs functioned okay, well, unless he tried to hurry. Then they sort of stiffened up on him. Nothing drastic, but it slowed him down more than he was used to before the back issues. He was working on that little drawback, however, the stiffness, by forcing himself to jog up and down med-bay. About half the length of a football field.

When he entered the seventh grade, he signed up to play football. He wasn't unfamiliar with sports. His family had moved to Iowa the year before, but in his former school he played some basketball. Three laps did him in and it took all his strength to stumble to a bed before his legs gave out.

Still…progress.

An hour later, Cujo wolfed his lunch, mushroom and Swiss burger and fries, sucked down a bottle of water and said, "Fuck it."

He placed his tray on the bed and stood, ready to leave the med-bay, though didn't make it very far.

The med-bay doors whooshed open and Kirby Ross, Dr. Rollings and Connor entered the bay.

Cujo stopped and held up a hand. "Look, I gotta get out of here. I can walk just fine and—"

"Relax, Cujo," Ross said and smiled. "We have a proposal for you."

"More like a request," Dr. Rollings said.

Cujo glanced from Ross to Rollings and back again. "What are you talking about?"

Ross clasped his hands behind his back. "We request you go on a vacation."

"Doctor's orders, actually," Rollings said.

Cujo frowned. "Vacation? What about the team and—"

"They'll be going with you," Ross said. The tall, scrawny man chuckled, unclasped his hands from behind his back and stepped closer to Cujo. "I think you all need a bit of a recharge. Booked hotel rooms in Baja for a couple of weeks. All expenses paid, of course. Including food and whatever fun things you want to do."

"What about the cryptids? Reece said something about Australia when we talked a few days ago."

Ross nodded. "Yes. Australia needs our attention. I will send out a small team to capture intel. But I don't what you to worry about it for now." Ross turned away and began walking toward the doors.

Rollings did the same, but Connor remained where he stood.

"Oh," Ross said and spun around as the doors opened. "You leave in four hours." He flashed Cujo a smile and walked out of the med-bay.

Once the doors shut, Connor shrugged. "I mean, they're not wrong."

Cujo sighed and looked away. "I haven't had a real vacation in almost twenty years."

"Well, good time to take one now, right?" Connor said. "While you're healing?"

Cujo grunted, nodding. "Guess so." He lifted his head and frowned at Connor. "Baja? I don't think I've ever heard of it."

Connor blinked. "You've never heard of Baja, Mexico? Seriously?"

"Yeah. Seriously. Well, maybe in a movie or something." Cujo mulled it over a bit longer. "Yeah, some movie. One of those romantic comedies, I think."

Connor chuckled and sat on one of the beds. "You might want to look it up. Personally, I think it will be perfect for you to relax and heal up. All that hot sun and sand."

Cujo cringed. "Hot sun? I'm not a fan of—"

"And tequila," Connor quickly added.

Cujo snorted. "I'm more of a whiskey guy. Rum, if all else fails."

"Well, it is considered the tropics, right?" Connor brought up his tablet and tapped on it. "Bet they have some good local rum."

"I don't know. I think it's best I just stay here and—"

Connor shot off the bed and held the tablet out in front of him so Cujo could see the screen. "Look."

Cujo looked at the picture for a while, maybe a minute, he couldn't be sure, and straightened. He cleared his throat. "And?"

Connor flapped his arms, tablet still in hand. "*And*? It's beautiful, Cap. Why not take a couple of weeks off there? You deserve some rest, right? Said so yourself, you haven't had a vacation in almost twenty years. Don't you think it's time? With your age—"

"My *age*," Cujo said, instantly pissed off. "What about my *age*?"

Connor shrugged. "You're in your sixties."

"So?" Cujo stepped closer, daring the younger man to say the wrong thing.

Connor smiled. "You're like my dad, you know? If anyone mentions your age pertaining to why you can't do certain things or are slower, all of that...you get mad." He held up his hands. "I'm not making fun. Just an observation. And my dad can still whoop my ass, by the way."

Cujo's fists slowly relaxed and he sighed. "You about got a fistful in the face, kid."

"Oh," Connor said, "I know. Dad about tossed me over a cliff at the Grand Canyon one summer when he got winded from walking too much and I asked him how fifty was treating him." Connor chuckled. "Wrong thing to say to an old Marine still capable of tearing your head off."

Cujo tried holding it in, but it was no use. He burst out laughing. Laughing, even though what Connor said wasn't all that funny. Maybe it was just the stress of everything.

Maybe...Ross and Rollings made a good call.

"Vacation," Cujo said. He shook his head and walked over to his bed. On the nightstand was a single coin. A 1940 Third Reich coin his great grandfather gave him on his tenth birthday.

He picked the coin up and sat on his bed. The coin was still shiny after all these years and glimmered under the florescent lights.

Cujo glared at the swastika and the gravely voice of his great grandpa filled his head. "Wanna know why I kept that piece of trash? Hmm? B'cause it was a reminder, boy. A reminder there are evil men out there. Real monsters. All of 'em and all who follow 'em. I'm givin' this to ya so it will remind you too. Don't let the monsters win."

He sat on his bed and nodded. The coin had nothing to do with vacation, but there were other memories with his great grandpa. Those were the happy ones. Of long summers spent at a campground in northern Minnesota. Fishing from the early morning until noon. Sitting around the campfire while Great Grandpa told little Arron silly stories about squirrel monkeys in the trees and more serious stories of his time fighting the Nazis. All those mornings stepping out of the camper and breathing the fresh scent of pine mingling with the savory aromas of bacon and eggs. The mornings were always a bit chilly, but once he sat by the fire, the chills melted away.

Cujo smiled at the surge of memories.

Vacations. He had forgotten how beautiful they could be.

"Okay," Cujo said and stuffed the coin in his pocket. "Vacation it is."

Connor grunted back to Cujo, "Took you long enough to come around."

But Cujo wasn't really listening. Instead, he stood and got ready to leave.

SEVEN

The moment he stepped out of the airport and into Baja, California/Mexico's, savage heat, Cujo almost said, "Fuck it," and flew back to Iowa.

It was Wade who changed his mind.

"Damn, it's hotter here than I thought," Wade said as they stowed their gear (clothes, toiletries, and weapons) into the back of a black cargo van.

"Yep," Cujo said, wiping sweat from his face and forehead and stuffing the case containing his AC-900 into the crammed back section of the van.

"But I have a good feeling about this place," Wade continued. They walked around to the side of the van where the sliding door stood open. "We've been beaten around by zombie yetis, about eaten by Jersey Devils...I think we need this. Heat be damned. I think we just need to relax for a bit. R and R is always a good thing, right?"

Cujo nodded. "Right. Let's get to the hotel before my pasty Iowa ass melts out here."

Each member of the team had their own room, which catered to individual tastes from what Ross told them before departing. Therefore, Cujo's fridge was stocked full of beer, ribeye steaks, shredded Colby jack cheese, bacon, eggs, and milk. The cupboards held cereal, tortilla chips, and coffee. Ten cases of water were stacked in a narrow pantry. The furniture was plain with a TV, though Cujo didn't watch much television, he just liked the background noise. The bed was queen-sized.

He sighed, placed his clothes in the dresser under the TV and made sure his guns were snugged under the bed so that a cleaning person wouldn't stumble upon them. Ross hadn't wanted them taking weapons but lost that short battle. It was Reece who tipped the scales by telling Ross they would all feel safer with the weapons. Just in case...

He opened the French doors to the balcony and stood a moment, taking in the hot, salty air of the Pacific Ocean. The more he stood there, however, the more he noted. The different aromas and sounds. Grilled meat. A sharp spice he couldn't identify but tingled his nostrils. Sweat. People spoke from every direction. Some in English, most in Spanish. There was laughter and hooting. Somewhere within it all, a baby cried.

Cujo smiled despite himself. He ignored the trickle of sweat running down the side of his face and just took in the essence of Baja, Mexico. Salty and sweet and spicy. And, for just a moment, he could see himself living here. Maybe in a nice little home away from everyone with his own beach and fishing boat. Maybe…

Heavy knocking jarred him from his thoughts. He spun and drew his pistol in a single, fluid motion. Fluid, except for the twinge in his back. A reminder he needed to settle down. Relax.

"Ready, Boss?" Benny called from the other side of the door.

Cujo blew out a breath, holstered his pistol, and opened the door.

Benny, dressed in a bright Hawaiian shirt and strake white shorts, greeted Cujo upon the door being opened. The guy wore aviator sunglasses and a straw-like cowboy hat. He looked every bit the tourist, in other words.

"Luna found a nice cantina not far." Benny gave Cujo a once over. "You're goin' out there like that?"

Cujo, wearing a blue tank top and jeans, didn't see a problem. "Looks like it, right?"

Benny snorted. "You're gonna die of heat stroke before the day is out, Boss."

Cujo shrugged, made sure the keycard to his room was in his wallet and motioned for Benny to step away. He shut the door and walked toward the elevators.

"That's it," Benny said, catching up to Cujo. "I'm taking you shopping for shorts."

"No, you're not," Cujo said and pressed the down button for the elevator. "Let's get some beer."

Benny snorted. "We're supposed to drink fruity drinks, man. Margaritas. Daiquiris. You know, tropical stuff."

They entered the elevator and the doors dinged shut.

Cujo pressed the button for the lobby and turned to Benny. "That's nice. You can drink those. I'll have a beer."

"Well," Benny said, crossing his arms and leaning back against the wall of the elevator. "Well, ain't this going to be a fun time." He sighed and rolled his eyes.

Cujo chuckled. The elevator dinged and they stepped out.

"Give me a bit to adjust to this whole vacation thing, okay."

Benny sighed again. "Fine. But if you get heat stroke, remember, I told ya so."

The rest of the team sat waiting in the lobby. All of them wore shorts and colorful tank tops.

Maze glanced at Cujo, then at Benny. "He knows he's supposed to wear shorts, right?"

Benny flapped his arms in exasperation. "I tried telling him."

Cujo laughed and walked to the tall glass doors of the hotel. "Well, let's get this vacation started."

"Such a party animal," Benny murmured.

And Cujo laughed some more.

EIGHT

The heat proved to be too much for Cujo.

After visiting a few small shops, and sweating beyond belief, he broke down and bought a couple of pairs of cargo shorts before they all headed to a nearby cantina for some lunch and much needed cold drinks.

Cool air kissed Cujo's sweat-slicked skin the moment they entered the place. Mingling aromas of onions, cooked beef and spices tickled his nostrils. The lighting was dim to the point of soothing, not creepy. A woman stood on the opposite side of a long bar, smiling while she dried a glass mug. A huge mirror sprawled out behind her, wall to wall. Thirty feet, give or take, Cujo reckoned. A shelf made of gray bricks also stretched the same length and on it, lined up like sentinel soldiers, were hundreds of liquor bottles. Every brand Cujo knew about, and some he'd never heard of.

She didn't say anything for a minute or so, until they approached the bar.

"¡Hola amigos! Bienvenido a Baja Cantina. ¡Lo mejor de la ciudad! ¿Bebidas primero?"

Cujo blinked. They stopped and glanced at each other.

"Uh," Benny said. "Anyone speak Spanish?"

"She said, 'Hello friends! Welcome to Baja Cantina. Best in town! Drinks first?'" Ellen stepped beside Cujo.

He frowned at her.

Ellen smiled and shrugged. "Studied Spanish in high school."

"I mean," Luna said, "I did too, but can't remember anything, really, besides the small stuff."

Ellen chuckled. "I might have studied a few years after, too."

"Cute and bilingual," Maze spouted. "I knew I snagged a good one."

Ellen smiled, though Cujo noted a slight bit of discomfort. Nothing major. A slight furrow between the eyes. There and gone. Either discomfort or annoyance.

Ellen held up a finger to the woman and the woman nodded. She never really stopped smiling. Ellen turned to the team.

"What do you all want to drink?"

She went down the line, relaying their English drinks in Spanish to the bartender who nodded and went to work. In no time, they had their drinks lined up on the bar.

Cujo placed down what he thought might be enough to pay for the drinks - Ross had given them each a considerable amount of pesos to spend on food and whatever else they wanted to do on their vacation.

The woman counted the pesos carefully, paused, frowned, and counted the notes again.

She looked at Cujo and said, "Mil cuarenta pesos. No noventa pesos."

Ellen sighed, "She said, 'One thousand forty pesos. Not ninety pesos.'"

"Oh," Cujo said and coughed up the rest.

"Really, Boss?" Benny said. "You're gonna stiff a bartender?"

"I've never worked with pesos before, dickhead. Fuck off."

Benny, straddling a wooden stool in front of his drink, some multicolored madness, laughed and then took a strong pull from the straw of his drink. He leaned back a bit, sighed and grinned at Cujo.

"I might just stay here now, Boss. Get yourself another sniper."

They all sat at the bar, drank their drinks and ordered their food, the latter with the help of Ellen, of course.

Cujo finished his lunch, chugged down his third beer and said, "We got all week. Why not rest the first night in our rooms?"

They sat at their own private table on barstools Cujo hated and stared at him as though he had a booger dangling out of one of his nostrils, or something.

"What?"

They glanced at each other then looked back at him.

Maze leaned forward. "You know it's only like four in the afternoon, right?"

Cujo stretched his back. It didn't give him any pain. Just stiff from sitting too long on a barstool. A normal feeling he appreciated after weeks of pain by simply moving.

"I know," he said and stood. He backed away from the bar a bit, stomach full, vision blurring around the edges. He needed sleep. Jetlag sucked fuzzy donkey balls. "Maybe a nap, then?"

For the first time, they appeared genuinely concerned. He was usually the driving force of the team. But now...

Now...

Cujo sighed. "You guys go have fun. I'll meet up with you at the beach in a couple of hours."

Benny opened his mouth, and closed it again. They all nodded.

"I'll go back with you," Ellen said.

"What?" Maze said. "Why?"

Ellen shrugged and walked toward Cujo. "I could use a siesta." She smiled at Cujo. He smiled back.

Maze frowned. "Okay. See ya two later then, I guess."

"Don't get too fucked up," Cujo said. "We have all week, remember?"

His team, his family, all groaned and nodded as though they were children mad about not being able to go on all the rides at Disney World in a single day. They, apparently, didn't know about savoring a moment. A week was a short time in the grand scheme of things, but it could also rejuvenate and keep it shining a bit longer. At least that's what he believed anyway.

Cujo gave them a wave and exited the cantina with Ellen.

The heat struck him like a meaty fist to the gut, nearly doubling him over.

"You okay?" Ellen asked.

He grimaced. "Yeah. Just not a fan of the heat."

She nodded and walked ahead a bit. "I hear that. I would've been happier in northern Maine or Minnesota than down here."

Cujo matched her pace and wiped sweat from his forehead. "Me too. It's tropical here, even if people claim it's dry heat. Humid enough for me, anyway. I like a cool breeze every now and then."

"Same," Ellen said.

The rest of the walk to the hotel, about three blocks, give or take, they didn't speak much, and it dawned on Cujo how little he really knew about Ellen.

"You used to live in Maine or Minnesota?"

She smiled. "Both, actually." She looked straight ahead. "My dad was a piece of shit. A drunk. A drug addict. He'd hurt me or my mom, or both, every night. Or so I remember, anyway. All in Minnesota that happened."

"Oh, hell," Cujo said, heart breaking for Ellen. He hated to hear personal stories like this. Some men were just evil. Plain and simple. No gray areas. "I'm sorry."

Ellan waved a hand at him. "The past. It was horrifying in the house, but outside…there were lakes and tall pine trees. There was the smell of sap and green. A light, fresh scent. A soothing scent, I guess. Only thing like it was in Maine. My biological boogeyman went to prison, and Mom moved us to Maine. I was around twelve."

Cujo opened one of the double doors to the hotel for her. "I know the feeling. The soothing scent." He fell in behind her as they entered the hotel. "Northeast Iowa was like that for me. So was Minnesota when I lived there growing up. That smell…" He shook his head. "Always felt like home."

They walked by the lobby desk to the elevators and Ellen shot him a look he couldn't quite read, though he noted the slight smile.

"What part of Minnesota?"

He grunted. "Northwest. A couple hours east of Fargo, North Dakota."

As they entered an elevator, Ellen said, "We lived near the Canadian border. Lake of the Woods wasn't far if I remember right."

The ride to the fifth floor of the hotel was in silence. Cujo wasn't sure what to say. He'd learned a bit more about Ellen in just a few minutes than he had in the couple of years he had known her. He felt shitty about that. But, then again, Ellen was more the quiet type. Only one she really talked to was Maze. They seemed to be in a casual relationship, though lately not so much. Ellen always appeared distracted these days.

The elevator doors swooshed open and they stepped onto their floor.

"Thanks for the chat, Cap," Ellen said and walked down the hall toward her room.

He smiled. "Anytime."

In his room, he kicked off his shoes and plopped onto his bed. Before his mind could find much thought, he was asleep.

NINE

He woke to the shrill ring of the phone on the nightstand.

Cujo groaned, rolled over onto his back and squinted at the ceiling. At first, he had no idea where he was. But, as the phone continued its annoying bray, it all came back to him.

Hotel. Baja, Mexico.

Right.

He sat up, stretched and answered the phone. "Hello?"

"Jesus Christ," Benny said. "I was about to come break your door down. Thought you keeled over on us."

Cujo stretched his neck from side to side. "Why?"

"Boss, I've been tryin' to call you for almost an hour."

Cujo blinked. He glanced around but couldn't find a clock. "What time is it?"

"About six-thirty in the afternoon, man."

"Shit," Cujo said and stood. "I'll be right down." He hung up before Benny could say anything further.

He took a leak, changed into one of his new pairs of shorts, slipped on his shoes, made sure his pistol was secure and hidden well under his shirt, and hurried out of his room.

Same as before, they all waited for him in the lobby.

"Gah," Maze said. "'Bout time, Pops. I'm withering away to nothing here." She patted her flat stomach clad in a yellow tank top.

Cujo grunted and glanced at them. "Well, let's get some chow, then."

Luna hopped up from one of the couches. "Tacos!"

The rest of the team gave a collective groan.

They might be from different military backgrounds, but in this team, they were themselves. A disjointed family.

"What?" Luna said. "You guys don't like tacos now?"

Cujo chuckled and walked toward the doors. "We'll find a place for everyone."

"Better have some burritos," Wade said.

Another collective groan.

"What?" Wade said. "I like burritos."

They moved out into the heat, which hadn't, as far as Cujo remembered from earlier, lessened one bit. Indeed, he started sweating the moment he stepped out into the sun.

A sigh drifted out of him and he said, "Pick a place quick, kiddos."

"Yeah, for fuck sake," Benny spouted. "He's about to melt, people!"

Cujo rolled his eyes and walked faster, though he noted how the heat wasn't affecting him as badly as before. The more they walked, the more he noted a soft breeze kissing his sweaty forehead, which cooled him down a bit. He took to the edges of the street because in the shade of the colorful buildings the breeze was divine. Not quite the cool breezes during summers in northern Iowa, but close enough.

Maybe he would be okay here after all for the next week.

They soon found a nice little restaurant serving the best Mexican cuisine. Ellen said it was called Pops, which made Maze snort.

"Perfect spot for ya," Maze said and nudged Cujo.

He chuckled as he pressed the thumb latch down and pushed open the door. Instantly, a plume of cool air greeted him. At least ten degrees cooler than outside. Enough to make him both shiver and smile. A great relief from the heat, even though his body was slowly adjusting to it. Very slowly.

They found a couple of booths and ordered their dinner along with a couple of rounds of drinks. Cujo even gave one of Benny's fruity drinks a go. Some strawberry and watermelon concoction he didn't mind at all. Pretty tasty stuff, to be honest. Not something he would drink all the time, but not bad.

Maze, Ellen, and Wade sat with Cujo while Benny and Luna took up the booth across the aisle. Eventually, though, Ellen got up and joined Luna and Benny. Cujo noted Maze's composure stiffen a bit. Her expression soured and she looked away.

Wade slurped down the remainder of his tropical drink, burped, and said, "Gotta pee. Be right back."

Cujo nodded, waited for Wade to shuffle away and leaned across the table. "You two okay?" He shifted his eyes in Ellen's direction.

Maze shrugged. "Who knows." She took a big swig from her beer, placed the mug down and smiled. "Not a big deal if we aren't. We'll still be friends and functioning members of the team."

"Oh," Cujo said. "That, I have no doubt." He straightened a bit. "She seems to be the one taking whatever is going on the hardest, though."

Again, Maze shrugged, though this time flashed a smile at Ellen in the other booth. Ellen didn't smile back, her face stuck in a frown.

Cujo nodded and let the subject fade into silence while they drank their beer and shoveled queso and chips into their mouths. It really wasn't any of his business and he sometimes forgot he was the leader of an elite team of monster hunters. Sometimes the family side of it distracted him more than it should.

He knew he should have gone with his gut and not gotten too close with everyone. Maybe he should just—

A loud crash jolted Cujo from his thoughts.

A young woman, maybe in her early twenties, stumbled into the restaurant. She tripped over her own feet and went sprawling onto the floor. The waiter, a scrawny man with thinning hair and a full, black beard, dashed across the room to her in a flourish of Spanish.

Cujo and the team stood from their booths.

"He's asking her what's wrong," Ellen said. She frowned. "Asking who she is and how he can help."

The young woman spouted a string of words at the man. Her eyes were wide, long, dark hair wet and dripping. The man helped her to her feet.

"She's saying something about a devil," Ellen said. "It's too fast, I can't get it all."

"Devil?" Benny said. "Uh-nope." He sat back down in the booth. "Had my share of devils, thank you."

"Shh," Ellen said, moving closer to the two.

"We're supposed to be on vacation, people," Benny said.

Ellen stepped closer yet while the distraught woman and the concerned man spoke.

"He's asking her what she means by the Devil," Ellen said. "She says: the devil of these waters."

The waiter let go of her shoulders and she would have dropped to the floor if not for Ellen, who swooped her up and placed her gently in a nearby booth.

The male waiter shook his head and shouted something at the young woman.

"He's asking what kind of drugs she's using and if he needs to call for medical help," Ellen said.

Cujo moved to Ellen's right side. "It's not drugs. She saw something that scared her." His jaw clenched while the woman's lower lip quivered, and her wide eyes shifted back and forth. He saw about the same reaction in many of the women and children in every war and mission he helped fight.

"I know," Ellen said.

"Hey," Wade said somewhere behind Cujo. "What's going on, guys? Still got another round of drinks."

It was obvious Wade wasn't much of a drinker. One of the fruity drinks had his voice a bit slurry.

"Shh," Benny said. "They're engaged in a game of what the scared girl is saying."

"Huh?"

Benny sighed. "Never mind. Here, finish your drink, Wild Thing."

"Wild Thing? I don't—"

"Will you two shut up," Maze said.

For a wonder, they did. Cujo returned his attention to the scared woman and waiter.

"I can't make out what she's saying," Ellen said. "She's about to cry and speaking too fast, but I think she said 'devil' a few times and 'in the water'."

The waiter spun away from her and stormed to a phone near the small bar and a cash register. He dialed a number, all the while frowning at the distraught woman.

"Let's get her out of here," Cujo said. "I don't think he's calling for medical attention."

"Cops," Ellen said. "He doesn't believe her and thinks she's on drugs."

Cujo hurried to the woman, Ellen matching his stride. The woman glanced from Cujo to Ellen and back again. She muttered something and began backing away.

Ellen said something in Spanish and the woman stopped. She frowned and said something back in return making Cujo wish now more than ever he had paid more attention in Spanish class in high school.

Ellen nodded and turned to Cujo. "She's skeptical but will go with us."

Cujo tossed a wad of money on the booth table and gestured for the rest of the team to follow him, Ellen and the woman out of the restaurant.

None of them hesitated.

The waiter's angry shouts followed them out until the door slammed shut, cutting off his tirade.

The woman refused to talk until they were far away from the restaurant. Even then, she merely whispered to Ellen as they walked under canopy after canopy. It wasn't until they found a secluded spot under a palm leaf hut near the beach when she began speaking in earnest.

"So," Maze said, sitting down at a round table Cujo assumed was built out of driftwood. "What the hell is going on?"

The salty ocean breeze swept into the hut. Cujo winced, not at all liking the briny taste on his lips and the tingle in his nostrils. It reminded him too much of all his tours overseas. The horrors…

"She's been telling me about her day," Ellen said. "She's a fisherman's daughter and was out on a boat with a few of her father's crew to catch some mahi-mahi for the season, but they found debris from another boat." Ellen paused. "That's about all she's told me so far. She wanted to get to a place where no one could overhear our conversation."

Benny sighed. "So, she chose a sweat hut. Because of course she did. Gah."

"Shut it, Benny," Cujo said, even though he agreed with the guy. The hut was sweltering. He wiped sweat from his forehead and said, "What's this about boat debris?"

Ellen nodded and spoke in Spanish to the woman. Slowly. Clearly. The woman, hair now a frizzy mess, lowered her head, listening.

Eventually she said something to Ellen. Ellen nodded and patted the woman's hand across the table.

Ellen shot Cujo a glance. "She says it was the Black Demon."

"Black Demon?" Benny spouted.

"The fuck is that supposed to mean?" Maze said.

Ellen flashed Maze a glare and held up an index finger. A shushing gesture if ever Cujo saw one. She asked the woman something in Spanish.

The woman shrugged. Her gaze shifted to stare out the hut at the ocean. She spoke while Ellen translated.

"She says the Black Demon has been around for centuries. A scary tale passed down from one generation to the next." Ellen paused a bit, then continued. "She says her grandma told her such stories when she was younger. Of a giant monster waiting off the coast to snatch people and boats alike up."

Cujo frowned. "She thinks this Black Demon thing ate a boat?"

The woman was already talking before Cujo finished asking his question. Not as though she understood him, but rather going on about her story he was too impatient to know about.

"They came across the boat debris," Ellen translated. "But everyone thought it was from a storm to the north."

"I'm already bored," Benny said.

Cujo elbowed the kid, hard, in the ribs.

"Ow, dude, that—"

"Shut up," Cujo said. "You're a soldier. Act like one now."

Thankfully, Benny clammed up.

The woman, noticing Cujo correcting Benny, had stopped talking. Ellen smiled, patted the woman's hand and spoke softly in Spanish. The woman nodded, shoulders relaxing a bit. She sighed and waved a hand at the vast Pacific Ocean and spoke to Ellen. In turn, Ellen resumed translating.

"But it wasn't from the storm. Some of the debris had what they thought were bite marks. Big bite marks. Bigger than anyone had ever seen. One of the crew said the bite radius took up most of what he thought could have been a thirty-foot fishing charter."

"Is there anything in the ocean that big?" Luna asked.

No one answered her.

The largest predators in the ocean, as far as Cujo knew, were great whites and orcas. Sperm whales, maybe. But the only thing large enough to possibly have such a bite radius would have to be a megalodon. Couldn't be that, though. Megalodons were extinct.

The woman continued after a short pause. Ellen leaned forward, listening. Cujo caught a bit of Spanish he kind of recognized. "El Demonio Negro."

"Her name is Mary," Ellen said. "She's telling me how she never believed in the Black Demon until today."

"Did something attack her boat?" Cujo asked. "She was wet when she came into the restaurant."

Ellen spoke to Mary and the woman nodded, replying.

"Yes, but they got away before it could do any damage to the boat. It leaped out of the water, she says, and that's how she got wet. She thinks it couldn't damage their boat because it's bigger than the thirty-foot charter."

Cujo leaned back a bit, wiping beads of sweat from his forehead. A hot gust of salty air filled the hut. He swallowed and wished for a tall glass of ice water.

"The charter," Ellen said, still translating for Mary. "It was also one of her father's."

"So?" Maze said. "I feel like she's leaving something out."

Cujo nodded. He did too.

Ellen sighed and spoke to Mary slowly.

Mary straightened, blinked, and glanced around at everyone in the hut as though seeing them for the first time. She looked back at Ellen and spoke.

Ellen nodded and turned to Cujo. "She needs help. There's another charter out there. She says, last she knew it was low on fuel and trying to stay away from the Black Demon. But she needs to get to her father's docks to find out if the crew on that charter radioed in."

Cujo's jaw clenched. He wiped more sweat from his forehead. "Then we take her to her father and see what needs to be done."

"But aren't we on vacation?" Wade asked.

"That's what I said," Benny murmured.

"You two are being douches right now," Maze said. "Hope ya know that."

Benny waved a hand. "Yeah, yeah. Let's get this over with."

Mary led them out of the hut and turned south. They followed her in the glaring sun for about fifteen minutes before Cujo couldn't take anymore.

"Let's find some shade."

"C'mon, Pops," Maze said. "Use that military discipline."

He flipped her the middle finger and struck out on his own toward another beach hut.

"Mary says we're almost there," Ellen called after him.

He stopped, gritted his teeth, and returned to the team.

His throat screamed for water. Sweat trickled down his back to his ass crack. How anyone could live like this was beyond him. What he wouldn't give for a cool breeze every now and then sitting under a giant oak tree somewhere in northern Iowa.

It was the old memories of snoozing under the old oak behind the farmhouse that gave him strength to carry on. Of a much calmer life after all this Cryptid Force Six business. Retirement.

Carry on…

TEN

Mary's father was a stout man with thick, black hair and an even thicker beard. The office in which they all stood wasn't small. Indeed, it was as large as a twenty-foot by twenty-foot living room. In it, four people bustled around with papers, tapping on computer keyboards, while Mary's father sat at a small, steel desk shouting Spanish into a phone.

Despite the tension in the large office, Cujo caught the scent of strawberries. Someone's shampoo, perhaps? He glanced around but couldn't find an air freshener. Not even one of those plug-in types he had in his own home, well, the one he remembered, anyway.

Mary waited for her father to finish up yelling and slam the phone in its shallow cradle. He glanced from her to the team, gaze lingering on Cujo a moment longer than the others, before returning to Mary.

She spoke to her father and every now and then he'd look at Cujo.

Finally, he nodded, stood and smiled at the team. "Hola, amigos. Gracias por venir. ¿Quieres un poco de agua?"

"He says, "Hello, folks. Thanks for coming. Would you like some water?""

"Yes," Cujo said, wiping sweat from his face. "A couple bottles here, if he has enough."

Ellen translated and Mary's father nodded. He tapped a younger man on the shoulder who sat at a computer near the man's desk and spoke a string of Spanish.

The man stood and hurried out of the room.

Mary's father returned his attention to the team. "Mi nombre es Gabino García. Soy el dueño de la Carta de García. Veo que conociste a mi hija. Ella dice que puedes ayudarnos."

"He says his name is Gabino Garcia and he owns this charter service. He says Mary said we can help them." Ellen looked at Cujo. "Are we sure we want to get into this?"

Cujo sighed. "I don't know. Ask him what he needs from us."

Ellen translated this to Gabino who nodded right away and replied.

"He says, if we can help, he would like us to go out and find his missing charter."

"Missing?" Maze asked. "Mary over there said it was adrift, but not missing. What changed?"

Ellen spoke to Gabino. His eyebrows lifted and he pointed at Cujo.

"What?"

Gabino rattled something off in Spanish.

Ellen held up a quieting hand as Gabino continued talking. Cujo waited, wishing he could remember half the Spanish he learned in high school and a smattering of classes in the military. Those were mainly basic commands and questions, though. Nothing like a conversation.

"He says they last pinged the charter two hours ago about forty kilometers from the beach. Or twenty-five miles out." Ellen turned to Cujo. "Then it just disappeared. No communication from the charter's crew either."

"Then they're dead," Luna said. "Right?"

"Yup," Benny spouted. "Case closed. Look, if we hurry, we might be able to catch a few margaritas at that one bar with the live music. Saw a flyer at the hotel. El...something. We should—"

"Shut up," Cujo said as the man who hurried out earlier came bustling in with a cart and large bucket of ice with water bottles stuffed down to the necks.

Cujo yanked one of the bottles out, opened it, and drank the entire thing in a few seconds. He opened another and glanced at Ellen.

"Ask him why he thinks we can help better instead of local authorities," Cujo said.

Ellen translated the message while the others and Cujo drank more water.

After some time, Gabino nodded. He walked to the only window in the large room, gazed out onto his docks and remaining two charter boats and crossed his arms over his broad chest. A few seconds later, he began to speak while Ellen translated.

"I didn't catch the first couple of sentences," Ellen said. "But now he's saying he would rather have us out there than the local police because the police here can't be trusted. The Cartel has corrupted most of them and the last thing he wants is for the Cartel to be involved. When Mary told him about us, he knew what to do, if we should accept his offer."

Cujo frowned, and took a swig of water. "What offer?"

Ellen asked Gabino.

The man turned away from the window and looked directly at Cujo. Oh, yes, he could tell who the leader of the team was. *Clever*, Cujo thought, watching Gabino closely.

Gabino spoke something slowly in Spanish. His gaze never left Cujo.

"He says he will pay us five million American dollars to rescue his missing charter, kill the Black Demon and bring everyone home safely."

The office fell into a deep silence. So quiet, Cujo thought he could hear Benny's heart beating next to him. Or maybe it was his own...

Cujo cleared his throat and, still keeping eye contact with Gabino, nodded. "Tell him we're not mercenaries and will need to get ahold of our employer before committing."

Ellen relayed the message.

Gabino smiled, nodded and said a couple of words Cujo recognized. "Gracias, amigos!"

"Wait," Benny said and pulled Cujo away from Gabino and the others. Cujo rarely caught the younger man frowning and right now Benny was indeed frowning.

"What?"

Benny sighed, glanced over his shoulder to make sure no one was listening, and faced Cujo. "You're gonna pass up five million bucks? Just like that?"

Cujo clenched his jaw. He didn't answer for a few seconds. When he did, he made sure to control his tone. "What part of we're not mercenaries did you not understand?"

"I know that, Boss, but c'mon. It's five *million*. And all we gotta do is get that charter, kill a shark and come back? Sounds like a pretty fucking easy way to make some side cash while on vacation to me."

Cujo blew out a slow breath and looked away. When he returned his gaze to Benny, he made sure his face told the kid everything he needed to know about his response. "No."

Benny blinked at Cujo for a moment, then let go a wheezy chuckle. "Boss, look. If we—"

"How long have you been under my command?"

Again, Benny blinked. He stepped back a bit, frown deepening.

Cujo stepped closer. "How long?"

"A-Almost fifteen years. I think. Maybe lon—"

"Twenty years and six months," Cujo said. "*Twenty* fuckin' years, kid. And in all that time, did I ever strike you as the kind of man who would accept money over duty or morals?"

"Well…" Benny said. "Weren't we offered money to kill those yetis?"

"Money I turned down," Cujo said. "Kirby Ross is our employer. We don't work for big paydays. We work to save lives from violent creatures. Before that, we worked to save lives from terrorists and bad motherfuckers. Remember?"

Benny sighed and lowered his head. Eventually, he nodded. "Yeah. Okay."

Cujo leaned in close so the others wouldn't hear. "We do good, brother, for the sake of good. We fight for those who can't. That's what it's always been about. Not you or me. We do what others can't."

For a few seconds, Benny kept his head lowered. A long sigh blew out of him. "Yeah." He cleared his throat and straightened a bit. "Yeah. Sorry, Boss. You're right. I didn't join the Army for shits and giggles."

Cujo clapped the man on the shoulder. "I know, kid. Let's get ahold of Ross and see what we can do here."

Benny grunted. "Man, this vacation sucks."

ELEVEN

Back at the hotel, they crammed themselves into Cujo's room while Dr. Reece and Kirby Ross stared at them through a laptop screen.

"The Black Demon?" Reece asked.

"No," Maze said. "It's the blue one. *Yes*, the Black Demon."

Reece frowned. "Give me a sec." She disappeared from view, leaving everyone to stare at Ross.

The thin man adjusted his glasses. "So, other than the whole Black Demon thing, how's vacation going?"

Cujo stopped Benny from kicking the laptop and said, "Oh, ya know. All sunshine and margaritas." He pushed Benny away toward the door and turned back to Ross.

"Is there something wrong with Mr. Riley?" Ross said. "He looks kind of angry."

Somewhere behind Cujo, Benny mumbled something too low to hear, though Cujo caught something that sounded a lot like "pompous fucker".

"Once Dr. Reece has all the information collected," Ross said, "I'll send you whatever you need." He paused a moment, and scratched the back of his head. "Um, any of you have diving experience?"

The team glanced around at each other.

Ross blinked. "I'll take that as a n—"

"Yes," Ellen said. "Haven't done it since SEAL dive training and exercises a few years ago, but I think it'll all come back to me."

"Jesus Christ," Maze said. "Ms. Jack of All Trades over here."

Ellen shot a glare at Maze, sighed and returned her gaze to Ross. "We should be fine as far as diving goes, but it will take time to train everyone."

Ross nodded. "Time, it seems, we don't have. I do have special dive suits I acquired about four years ago. All proven exceptionally durable and self-sustaining. Invented and used by an old oil digger named Bracken Tull, I believe. Fought a creature I'm still keeping my eye on. A real leviathan."

"You really think we'll need those suits to kill a shark?" Luna said and stepped forward a bit. "I—"

"The Black Demon shark," Reece said, "is reported to be at least fifty feet long. Said to be a direct descendant of the megalodon, though nothing has been confirmed on that. The last documented encounter with the shark, a few years ago, ended in the death of twenty people on a personal yacht a few miles from the beaches of Baja. There wasn't much left of the yacht except some debris and massive bite marks. No bodies were found."

"So," Wade said. "We're really going after a fifty-foot shark that might or might not be goddamn megalodon?"

"Not confirmed a megalodon, my dude," Benny spouted.

"I know that," Wade said. He shot a glare at Benny. "But is this even a cryptid?"

"So what if it isn't?" Luna said. "It's killing people, right? I think we should at least check it out."

"I—"

"It's a cryptid, Wade," Reece said. "Very little is actually known about the Black Demon. Most of its story is rooted in local folklore. Skin black as midnight and piercing eyes somehow even darker. It's said to overturn boats, attack whales, and swallow groups of sea lions whole. It has a long tail, which creates large waves on the surface. There is no physical or photographic evidence the Black Demon exists, but locals believe the half-eaten whale carcasses that wash ashore are because of the Black Demon. There is typically only one bite. Typically, the radius of those bites are around fifteen feet."

No one said anything for about a minute or two.

Finally, Cujo sighed. "So, this thing has been here a long time?"

"Centuries, according to legend," Reece said. "About as much history as the yeti from Asia."

Cujo nodded. "Then let's get this done."

"All equipment will be implemented with upgrades to deal with the potential danger," Reece said. "This might be our very first underwater mission. I'm going to take every precaution necessary."

"When should we expect equipment to arrive?" Cujo asked.

"Three days," Reece said. "I need time to implement the adjustments in software. I'll also be bringing on a team who know more about the marine mech suits."

"Who?" Cujo asked.

She glanced down for a moment, then looked at the camera and the team. "Devil Divers. A team who has extensive knowledge of these deep-sea suits."

Cujo nodded. "What's their ETA?"

"I just dispatched them," Ross said. "They have their own jet. Really fast model, from what they tell me. Should be a little over an hour for arrival."

"That's a damn fast jet," Maze said.

"One of their own inventions," Ross said. He smiled. "Bastards. Wish I would've thought of that."

"What the fuck are you—"

Someone shut Benny up before Cujo could turn and do it himself. He could assume what the younger man was about to say. What the fuck are you talking about? You're already rich, for shit sake.

Yes. Cujo could see that going very badly on their end. Could see Ross booting Benny from the team.

"What was that?" Ross said. He appeared genuinely concerned. As if he missed some important detail in a meeting.

"Benny is playing games on his phone again," Maze said.

"Fuckin' Fortnite," Benny said, voice grumbly. Not his usual chipper self.

Cujo wasn't liking this side of the man. There would be words later.

"I don't believe I've ever played that before," Ross said.

"Well, you're not twelve so…" Maze said.

"Shut up," Benny said.

"Suck my dick," Maze said.

Cujo snorted and glanced at her over his shoulder. She smiled and waved. He shook his head and looked back at Reece and Ross on the laptop screen. Both appeared a bit perplexed.

Cujo shrugged and said, "Just kids being kids."

"Ah," Ross said, still frowning. "Well, then." He adjusted his posture a bit. "The equipment will arrive within three hours. The Devil Divers should be there within the hour. Gives you guys some time to get acquainted."

"I'm sorry but," Luna said out of nowhere, "we don't need another team interfering."

"They are being sent to simply train you how to use the deep-sea suits," Ross said. "Nothing more."

"And if they try to interfere?" Cujo said.

"Then you let me know immediately and I will remedy the situation." Ross leveled his gaze on Cujo. "Do not try to remedy it yourself. I require respect from both teams. Their funder agrees with this also."

"Who's their funder?"

Ross shook his head. "I can't say. But I do know her, and she is fair."

"The Garcias need help right now," Ellen said. "I don't think that missing charter has too much longer to wait."

"If it's the boat I'm pinging right now," Reece said, "then we might have a bit of time. It hasn't been long since the attack. The Devil Divers shouldn't take too long on how to operate the suits. Roughly four hours is my guess."

"Four hours to learn how to maneuver and use a state-of-the-art deep-sea mech suit?" Maze said. "That doesn't even feel possible."

"They've been instructed to give you a quick run-through," Ross said. "Their funder said she didn't think you would have to use the suits anyway."

Everyone fell silent for a bit, even Benny.

"Um, but what if we do have to use them?" Maze said.

"Then you'll know the basics," Ross said. He waved a hand. "The team are world renowned, Ms. Williams. I can assure you they're professional."

Cujo sighed, and leaned forward to shut the feed down. "We'll see."

"Cujo, don't—"

He tapped the end call button, cutting Reece off.

Truth was, he'd heard of the Devil Divers before. They had a certain kind of...reputation...

Nothing good, either. Well, except for stopping monsters to save the world, of course. They were good in that sense, but otherwise...

Cujo stood and faced his team. "Get ready for some bullshit."

TWELVE

Cujo recognized Brax Miller the moment he sauntered into the hotel lobby. The crooked smirk. The tall, lanky frame of a gunslinger. The icy blue eyes which never seemed to leave Cujo. His thick black was in the same swept back style the bastard always sported.

"Well, hell," Brax said in his usual booming voice. A sound which made Cujo's hands instantly clench into fists. He loathed loud people. Especially the big male bravado type. There was absolutely no reason to bellow all the time.

Brax held out a hand for Cujo to shake as he approached. "Been a minute, hasn't it, Captain Wright?"

Cujo shook the man's hand and nodded. Everyone in the lobby stared at them.

"Yep," Cujo said, hating all the attention on him. "Follow me."

Brax chuckled but didn't follow Cujo. Rather, he matched Cujo's pace, and they walked side by side to the elevators.

"So, you got yourself a monster killin' team too, huh?"

"Something like that," Cujo said and pressed the up button for the elevator.

Brax snorted. "Somethin' like that, huh? Well, what is it y'all do then?"

The elevator dinged and the doors swooshed open. Without answering the man, Cujo stepped into the elevator.

Brax followed and leaned against the wall opposite Cujo, smiling. The man had an almost predatory smile. Something hungry in it. It always unnerved Cujo.

"Kinda quiet, Captain."

Cujo pressed the button for the sixth floor. The doors closed.

"Not much to say," Cujo said. He turned to Brax. "Where's your team?"

Brax shrugged. "Gettin' a margarita or six, I reckon."

Yes. Pretty much everything about Brax Miller resembled a gunslinger from the Old West. Right down to the way he spoke.

Cujo nodded. "Shouldn't they be here too? We don't have much time."

Brax's icy stare melted some. "I know, Captain. I know. They'll be waitin' for us after this meetin'. We'll get ya fixed up and ready to kick ass."

For the first time, Cujo saw the real person behind Brax's tough guy persona. It took him aback a bit to see it. In the end, however, it was a relief. Maybe the guy wasn't really the asshole Cujo remembered from a few years ago.

The elevator dinged, and the door opened on the sixth floor.

Cujo gestured for Brax to go ahead, but the son of a bitch shook his head and said, "Captains first."

Cujo sighed and stepped out of the elevator and into a room sporting a couple of vending machines. Slumped in the far corner of the room was an ancient ice maker. A sardonic clunk radiated from the old thing and water seeped from the far-right corner, creating a small pool on the floor. The fluorescent light flickered sporadically from a water-stained ceiling.

Brax clapped Cujo on the shoulder, startling the older man. Cujo's jaw clenched. When did he get so damned jumpy?

"Easy, pal," Brax said, stepping in front of Cujo and frowning. "Everything okay? You're a bit off. Old age make ya lose your edge?"

Before Cujo could reply, Brax continued.

"'Cause I've seen it, bud. Oh yeah. Gettin' old in this profession is the shits, ya know? I mean if—"

Cujo shoved Brax aside and walked away. "We don't have time for this."

Brax, thankfully, said no more until they entered the room.

"Jesus Christ," Maze said. "Took you two long enough to get back here."

Cujo frowned. "What's up?"

"Reece said she lost the ping."

"Ping?" Brax said. "The fuck ya talkin' about a ping?"

Cujo sighed, trying to focus on Maze. "So, we lost the charter?"

"Pretty much," Maze said.

"Oh, good," Benny said. "We can get back to our vacation now."

Cujo shot him a glare and Benny lowered his head.

"Then why are we here?" Brax said. His voice practically shook the hotel room.

"I'm sorry," Maze said. "Who the hell are you?"

Brax snorted. "Ah, shit. Sorry." He stepped forward and extended a hand. "Brax Miller. Former Master Chief for the Navy SEALs, now a goddamn monster killer, like yourself, Miss...?"

Maze didn't shake his hand. Instead, she glared directly into Brax's eyes. Cujo stepped back a couple feet. He knew that look. He was at the opposite end of it many times for a year or so...

"Call me Maze," Maze said, still staring the large man in the eyes. She was about a foot shorter, but that didn't stop her. She moved closer. "So, 'Master Chief', how long have you been hunting monsters?"

Brax chuckled. "Longer than y'all. That's for sure." He smiled, and it actually appeared genuine to Cujo. He glanced around at the team. "Look, I'm only here to teach y'all how to use my dive suits. No need to get your tightie-whities in a knot. Once y'all are ready, my team and I will book it back home."

Maze nodded and stepped back a few feet. The tension in the room petered out.

Cujo sighed and said, "We better get moving."

Brax grunted. "Then let's fuckin' do this." He brought a phone out from the front pocket of his jeans, tapped it a few times and snapped his gaze to the laptop. "That thing runnin'?"

"Yeah," Cujo said. "Why—"

"Oh shush, Captain. I'm just gonna hack into her."

"Hack into her?" Benny said. He started forward, but Luna and Ellen stopped him. He shook his head. "That's a private computer, man. You can't just hack into it. We might have some important shit there. Classified shit. You know, *only* for this *team*?"

Brax lowered the phone. His mouth split into a big, white smile. "Well, look at you." He chuckled. "Easy there, cupcake. I'm not gonna tell anyone about the donkey porn ya got stashed on here."

Benny blinked. Gradually, the corners of his mouth quirked. His chest shook and he burst into laughter. Once the laughing fit was over, he wiped his cheeks and eyes from tears and pointed at Brax.

"Okay, you're cool. Just don't steal all my porn while you're rooting around in there, eh?"

Brax winked. "Don't need to. Got my own collection at home."

"You guys," Maze said. "Yeah, see there's something wrong with both of you."

Cujo was still smiling at the antics when he said, "Okay, get on with it."

"Pushy, pushy," Brax said and tapped the phone a couple more times.

Suddenly the laptop screen flickered on, revealing a silhouette of a man on fire. Arms at his side, body at about a forty-five-degree angle aimed downward and in the form of a professional skydiver.

"Hey," Benny said. "How come we don't get a cool logo too?"

Cujo chuckled. "Put that in the suggestion box when this is all over."

Benny rolled his eyes. "Fine."

"Y'all always act like high schoolers, or is this like a friendship thing between y'all?"

"I wish I was in high school again," Benny spouted. "I was always getting laid."

Cujo shook his head. "That's enough. Brax…get on with it."

Brax nodded and turned to the laptop. "My suits are one of a kind and can't be replicated. There are none like them in the world. Close copycats, I reckon, but not the real deal." He tapped his phone and screen flipped from the team's logo to an image of the suit.

Cujo's team leaned closer to the laptop. It took Cujo a few seconds for his mind to wrap around the image. He expected something mech-like. Larger and not as sleek and refined. Indeed, it looked like something out of a science-fiction movie. A full body suit, complete with what appeared to be an attached helmet.

"This is my first suit. Rated depth for three-hundred-and-four meters." Brax shot a glance over his shoulder at Benny. "For the goobers in the room, that means one thousand feet."

"Hey…" Benny said. "Why'd you look at m—"

"This is Devil 1," Brax said. "It can withstand the pressure of one thousand feet and still perform flawlessly." He pointed at the shoulders, elbows, wrists, hips, knees and ankles. "As y'all can see, this ain't your typical mech. Though it *is* a mech suit. Mainly voice operated, but also allows you to move and intensifies those movements twenty times while underwater. Making you twenty times stronger than a silverback gorilla. The suit can also withstand the four thousand PSI of a great white shark bite. In the right arm, you have twelve mini missiles which will deploy two at a time unless the diver commands otherwise. Left arm is a high-end laser which lasts about half an hour."

Cujo, along with the rest of the team, gawked at the suit. It was so futuristic yet had a grounded appearance too. Grounded in this reality. A goddamn technological achievement, as far as Cujo was concerned. The suit itself looked almost form fitting, though according to Brax, while he highlighted features of the suit, it gave his largest team member, who stood almost seven feet and pure muscle, at least eight inches to move around without the suit touching her skin. Though Brax did caution that if anyone suffered from claustrophobia to not get in the suit.

Another feature Cujo admired was the lack of oxygen tanks. Rather, Brax told them, there were inlets, or gills, as he put it. These gills sucked water into a strange osmosis system Cujo didn't fully understand and flowed throughout the suit. The system drew the oxygen from the water, in other words, and expelled the water from tiny outlets like pores covering the suit. The oxygen gathered was then leaked into the suit for the pilot to breathe.

Listening to Brax explain everything gave Cujo yet another look at the real man. He invented these suits. This belligerent asshat created something no one else had. Well, as far as Cujo knew, anyway. There might be someone out there who invented something similar. Maybe they fought monsters too…

Whatever the case, Cujo might have been a bit wrong about Brax.

Although, an asshole was an asshole, after all. And Brax could definitely be an asshole. Their encounters were brief in the past, even before Cujo knew the man hunted monsters for a living. Brief, yet intense. They were polar opposites when it came to leadership. Cujo was a bit reserved, tough, but willing to let his platoon or team do their jobs without micromanaging.

Brax, on the other hand, he was balls to the wall constantly on everything.

Or, at least, he seemed that way.

Maybe it was all an act…

Brax finished his presentation and tapped his phone. The laptop screen turned black.

"If it's really the Black Demon," he said, "the bite force will be an estimated sixty times greater than that of a great white, so you're all vulnerable." He grunted. "Let's not be cute about it. If bites you, you're fuckin' dead, got me?"

Cujo and the team nodded, though Cujo couldn't escape the palpable sense of dread blasting through him. Maybe they should back away from this one. If the shark truly was so massive the thing would chomp them to bits as if they were nothing more than M&Ms. The mission was beyond them and they needed extensive training. They—

Hard, rapid knocking on the room's door crashed through Cujo's thoughts.

Before Benny could answer it, a tall woman built like Dolph Lundgren in his prime opened it and stepped into the room.

Benny stopped walking, turned to the team. "Anyone order a giant?"

The muscular woman rolled her eyes and shoved him aside. Benny stumbled into a dresser, rebounded, spun around and blinked at the woman. After a second or two, a smile spread along his whiskery face.

"I think I'm in love, guys."

The woman flipped Benny off and plopped down in the recliner near the only window in the room.

It was getting really crowded now, too. Cujo's anxiety crept up more than once and it took some doing to beat it back down while two more people stepped into the room.

An Asian woman and a black man with an easy smile on his face.

"Damn," the black man said. "This orgy is gonna be lit!"

"Oh, for fuck sake, Eb, keep it in your goddamn pants this time," Brax said.

Eb waved a hand at Brax. "Can't help it if they're all givin' me the sex eyes." He winked at Benny. "Especially you."

Benny snorted and turned to Cujo. "I like these guys."

Cujo sighed. "You hated them five minutes ago."

"Ten," Benny said. He shot a glare at Eb. "And it was the darkest ten minutes of my life."

Eb snorted, shook his head and tossed a duffle bag on the floor. "Think I found my fuckin' soulmate here, Jill."

The Asian woman behind him chuckled. "How many soulmates do you have now? Eighteen?" Even with the chuckle she appeared stern. A resting take-no-shit face if Cujo ever saw one.

Eb ruffled. "My god, no! What do you take me for, a slut? I—"

"Yes," Jill said and tossed her own duffle bag on the floor next to Eb's. "You're a slut." She faced Brax. "We ready to begin?"

Brax smiled. "Why, yes, darlin'." He gestured at Jill. "Folks, this is Jill Chow. Second in command of this little squad. Best deep-sea diver and biologist I ever had the pleasure of knowing." He pointed at the muscular woman in the recliner. "Over there is Jess. She's our enforcer and kicks all the ass, ain't that right?"

Jess shook her head and looked away.

Brax blinked, shrugged, and pointed at Eb. "Over there is Eden. We call'im, Eb. Former Coast Guard and my favorite intelligence dude. And, as y'all saw, quite the jokester."

"Jokester?" Eb blew a kiss to Maze and Wade. Both recoiled a bit, Cujo noted. "I'm just turned on, my dude."

Brax waved a dismissive hand at Eb. "Go find something to hump while we talk shop."

Eb chuckled and sat on the edge of the bed next to Benny. "Hey, pumpkin."

Benny laughed and shook the man's hand. They began talking among themselves while Brax and Jill addressed Cujo's team.

"Now that introductions are finished," Jill said. Her voice, strong and as sharp as a razor, cut through Benny and Eb's chatter. They both instantly fell silent. "Let's begin." She gained access to the laptop too and brought up images of a black shark, similar in appearance to a great white, though a bit bulkier.

"The Black Demon," Jill said and pointed at an image of a massive shark breaching the ocean's surface with what appeared to be a whale in its mouth. "This is a screenshot of a video from a fisherman about three months ago. The whale in its jaws is a fully grown humpback whale." Jill pointed at another image, though it was difficult to see at first what was going on. "Look closely here. This is diver Devon Mills, one of the best. He's posing for his friend at about one hundred feet deep a few miles south of Baja. Just a couple of friends goofing off for the day." Jill paused, then added, "Look at the background and tell me what you see."

Cujo leaned closer, focusing all his attention on the vast, murky blue behind Devon Mills. At first, he didn't see anything. Just the deep blue of the Pacific Ocean. Though, the more he focused, the better he saw it. And when he saw it he couldn't unsee it.

Shivers slithered like snakes along his spine and scuttled through his veins like tiny black spiders. He backed away, eyes widening.

"Fuck," Maze said, echoing the team's thoughts, as far as Cujo was concerned.

The more one stared at the image, the more the monster appeared through all that vast blue. A gradual change, like one of those Magic Eye books. A picture within a picture. Something lurking just below the surface.

All of that, but maybe the real reason was the thing was just so big compared to the man.

Cujo wasn't exactly sure how close the monster was, but too damn close would be his guess.

The massive head of a shark in profile took up all the lower half of the frame. All that darkness wasn't the deep. It was the Black Demon.

Cujo's heart stuttered. All the air leaked out of his lungs and his stomach churned.

"That's…" Luna said. "That's all shark below the guy?"

"Correct," Jill said.

"Fuck," Maze repeated from earlier.

Jill switched to a different image. This one made everyone but the Devil Divers wince. A man or woman stuck between the teeth of the Black Demon reaching out for help, eyes wide through the goggles. Blood clouded and obscured almost everything else.

"For Christ sake," Benny said. "You could've warned us!"

Brax grinned. He turned away from the screen and cocked his head at Benny. "Sorry. Did we hurt those feelers of yours, boy?" He moved closer and his grin lengthened a bit. Cujo got ready to intervene if shit hit the fan.

The air in the room intensified, as if infused with electricity.

Brax slowly paced back and forth. His body language was open and casual. The sign of a fearless person. Also, one who is rarely intimidated.

People like that were dangerous in Cujo's experience. Reckless. Sometimes murderous.

"Ya don't get what's under the surface, do ya?" Brax said, still pacing slowly. Still grinning after he spoke. "Hmm? Ever think to take a peek? Things swimmin' below ya can't even imagine."

Brax spun around and nodded at Jill.

She blinked, lowered her head, and tapped her phone.

The laptop screen flipped to an image of a massive, breaching shark with what appeared to be a yacht in its jaws. Floating in the forefront was the severed head of a woman. Her eyes revealed only the bloodshot whites. The tip of her tongue floated in the blue/green water and a deep gash across her forehead added to the cloud of blood in the water surrounding her.

"This is a screenshot of a social media live stream," Brax said. "The stream belonged to the friend of the woman's head you see shortly before the Black Demon crashed back down with that yacht and the feed died." He sighed and looked at every one of the Cryptid Force Six. His gaze lingered on Cujo for a moment. "I want ya to know what you're dealin' with here. Ain't just some big shark. This bastard will kill you just to kill you."

Cujo tore his sight away from Brax and settled his vision on the screen one last time.

He drew in a breath, blew it out slowly, and said, "Right. Guess it's time to put a stop to it then."

Brax smiled. "Well, now. That's the spirit, soldier."

THIRTEEN

"This is nuts," Benny said while the team stared at Brax's Devil 1 deep-sea suits. "We're going after a serial killer shark. We're supposed to be on vacation."

"Vacation or not," Cujo said, inspecting the suit standing in front of him, "this is what we do."

"But—"

"For Christ sake," Wade said. "Stop bitching, already."

"For real," Maze said. "Giving me a headache, dude."

Benny flipped Wade off. "Fuck off, you goddamn leprechaun. If I—"

"Enough," Cujo said, voice booming.

"It's time we start acting like professionals and I'll be damned if you all make us look like amateurs to Brax and his team." He shot each one of them a glare. "We're the Cryptid Force Six. Now let's do what we do best and kick ass. Enough fucking around."

Eventually, even Benny smiled.

"Damn, Boss. You go."

Cujo patted the suit and looked around. "Where the hell are they?"

"Brax?" Luna said. "Last I knew they were all having a beer at that little cantina about a block from the hotel."

Cujo clenched his jaw. "We don't have time for—"

Something heavy fell on his right shoulder and squeezed.

Cujo sucked in a sharp breath and spun away, tearing his shirt in the process. He landed hard in the sand as the dive suit stepped off its dock and off its low platform. Cujo scrambled to his feet.

"Holy shit," Benny shouted, helping Cujo back away from the moving suit.

Maze, Wade and Ellen drew their sidearms.

"Stop," Maze commanded.

The suit stopped walking and looked directly at her. It cocked its head, lifted its right arm, and pointed. Everyone froze. Somewhere close, a seagull screeched. The forearm of the suit whispered open and missiles about the length of a toothbrush slipped out, encircling the forearm. They rose about four inches away from the suit's arm so to avoid blasting a hand off, Cujo assumed.

Seconds staggered by like minutes. Cujo didn't dare wipe the sweat trickling down his face. If the suit was acting on its own, who knew what it would do to—

The helmet hissed open, lifting and then sliding backward, revealing Brax's grinning mug.

A burst of air blew out Cujo. He glowered at Brax. "What the hell do you think you're doing?"

Brax chuckled. "Havin' fun, Captain. Ya should try it sometime."

Cujo's hands curled into fists. "We're short on time and you're having fun?" He stepped forward a few paces. "Get the fuck out of that thing and show us how to use them so we can stop this killer shark."

Brax's grin withered. "Cryptid, Captain." He frowned. "This is not an ordinary shark, killer or otherwise. This monster doesn't always attack for food." The body of the suit opened like an Ironman suit and Brax stepped out onto the sand. "For all the intel we have gathered, Captain. This fuckin' monster enjoys killing. It loves destruction. And only every twelve years will it go on these sprees."

"Twelve years?" Ellen asked. "Mary thought it was always out there. A few occurrences happen every month."

Brax cocked an eyebrow at her while the rest of his team exited the other dive suits.

"Who's Mary?"

"Local woman," Cujo said. "The main reason why we're going to take it down. Her and her family business is suffering from a recent attack." Cujo frowned. "I thought Ross would have mentioned all that to you."

Brax smacked his forehead. "Oh, shit. That's right. The charter company. Guys, I'm sorry. When I go into story mode I kinda forget the other details."

Cujo and the team didn't say anything.

"But..." Brax began pacing again, that open body langue showing everyone he was not afraid of them. Not even Cujo. "Listen, kids, that thing has killed over three thousand people in the last couple of months. Y'all were so polarized after the yacht screenshot I didn't want to traumatize ya anymore."

Cujo noticed something interesting while Brax spoke. The more the guy got into what he was saying, the more belligerent, arrogant, and slang-ridden he became. It was like a Dr. Jekyll and Mr. Hyde moment.

Brax sighed. "Listen, kids. If I could go out there right now and kill the fucker, I would. But I got something else happening across the country in the Atlantic right now."

"What's going on in the Atlantic?" Ellen asked.

"Orgies," Eb spouted. "Island orgies. So many orgies!"

Brax shot Eb a glare and Eb shrugged. Brax sighed and looked at Ellen.

"We don't know yet. Something big. Possible kaiju."

"You mean," Benny said, "like in those big monster movies?"

Brax smiled. "Everything is inspired by something. Close enough."

"Then let's get this done so you guys can get back to your mission," Cujo said.

Brax chuckled. "Yes, Captain. Let's get this shit wrapped up." He straightened a bit. "Cryptid Force Six! I want you to stand in front of your suits."

When the team didn't move, Cujo gave them a nod. They all moved to the suits in front of them.

"If any of y'all get claustrophobic," Brax said, "say so now. These suits are close quarters."

"I do," Cujo said. "A little bit, anyway."

Brax nodded. "A little bit, he says?" He stepped next to Cujo's suit and patted its chest. "Ya think y'can live in this thing for over an hour, Cap?"

Cujo shrugged. "I don't know." Being honest. He had never been in something like that before. All he knew was he hated crawl spaces and tunnels so narrow he had to squeeze through in Afghanistan to find Bin Laden.

Brax smiled and Cujo immediately didn't trust the expression.

"You don't know?" Brax sauntered closer. He squinted. "Ya better be fuckin' with me."

Cujo straightened, glaring at Brax. "Stand down. I've never been in one of those things, so how would I know how I'd react?"

Brax stopped advancing and smiled. "Just keepin' ya on your toes, old man." He glanced at the Devil 1 and then returned his gaze to Cujo. "I think we should try it on for size."

The very thought of getting into the suit terrified Cujo. Tight spaces bugged the shit out of him. Still...

Cujo approached Brax. "Let's do this."

Brax cocked his head. "Yeah? Let's see what you're made of..."

FOURTEEN

"This is for basic operations," Brax said while he casually paced back and forth in front of them.

The sun baked the top of Cujo's head, and the salty sea air gave his throat a dry ache. He kicked himself for not grabbing a bottle of water before they came to the beach. He stared at the dive suit standing on the beach and shivered. Could he get inside that thing without anxiety crushing him?

There was only one way to find out.

"Basics," Brax said. "We'll walk you around the beach first. Get you accustomed to these bad bitches. Fair warning, though. They were meant for water, not land. You'll struggle. Then we'll get ya in the shallows for a few test runs."

"I thought this training was supposed to be quick," Benny spouted.

Brax stopped pacing and grinned. "Did I say how long each part would be, boy? No." His grin drooped into a glower. "Get in the fuckin' suit!"

The Cryptid Force Six all blinked in unison. Including Cujo.

"Did I fuckin' stutter? Sure as shit y'all aren't from the United States military if y'all can't understand simple fuckin' orders." He glared at each of the team members in turn. "Get your asses in the suits and let's get this done."

Cujo smiled when none of them moved. Brax glanced at him. A frown deepened on his face.

"Let's get this done," Cujo said, and his team moved to their suits, proving they knew who their leader was.

Brax grunted, smiled and gave Cujo a nod. He stepped aside and gestured for Cujo to approach his own suit.

"Try it on for size, Cap?"

Cujo sighed and walked to the suit. It loomed about two feet above over the top of his head.

He moved closer and Brax grabbed his arm. The man leaned close. "If, for any reason, you're uncomfortable in there, just say so and I'll hit the emergency release. I have a direct link inside each suit so I can hear y'all." He tapped the earpod in his right ear. "Don't hesitate, man. Seriously. No shame in it."

Cujo nodded, turned and stepped backward into the open suit.

Brax stepped in front of him. "Tell it to engage." A slight flash of what Cujo assumed was concern touched Brax's face. "Again, if you can't do it, just say so. I'll also be monitoring your heart rate."

"I'll be fine," Cujo said, and before Brax could respond, he added, "Engage."

The Devil 1 suit sucked him in and closed around him.

"Shit," Cujo managed while all kinds of lights and images popped up in front of him.

A bit of movement affirmed the few inches of space between flesh and the inside of the suit. It wasn't metal his elbow touched, though. More like soft padding.

"Give it a few seconds to adjust to your height and weight, Cap," Brax said through some hidden speaker in the suit. "How ya feelin'?"

The suit hissed around him and a one-hundred-and-eighty view screen slid in in front of his eyes. Suddenly he stared at the beach and the tops of some buildings.

"Cap?"

Cujo blinked. "Uh, yeah. So far, so good."

Truth. There was a bit of anxiety welling up in him, but nothing like he feared. Seeing outside of the suit definitely helped.

Brax stepped in front of him. The view was incredibly clear.

"Ya see me?"

"Yes."

Brax smiled and flipped Cujo the middle finger.

"Yeah, fuck you too, pal," Cujo said. "You going to teach us how to use these damn things or not?"

"Just makin' sure y'all are good before we get to it." He turned to the others. "Sound off when your suits adjust."

Down the line, each team member sounded off. Maze, Benny, Luna, Wade and Ellen.

"Good," Brax said. "This won't take long. The suits mimic every movement, stores that information in a data hub. Using that data, the suit can then anticipate your next move using the stored data. Comes in handy when you're down in the deep." Brax gestured at Cujo. "Each suit is linked to each other so ya can communicate freely and see what others in the team are seeing in real time."

"Sounds creepy," Benny said.

"Yeah?" Brax said, smiling in Benny's direction. "Wait till ya get separated from the others. Or ya need extra eyes. I'll tell ya, once ya get into the deep, ya can never have enough eyes looking out for you, son."

"Don't call me son."

Brax snorted. "Well excuse the shit outta me, kiddo. Ya wanna live through this? Might wanna fuckin' listen to the guy who invented these suits."

Benny didn't respond.

Brax beamed a smile at the team, stopping at Cujo.

"Now," he said. "Where the hell were we? Oh, yeah, extra eyes." He straightened a bit and the smile faded. "The suits are voice command and the more you talk, the better they will recognize you. So, we'll be doing a lot of talking during the land and water training. Anything special you want the suit to perform, all ya gotta do is say so. Like this..." He stepped out of view. "Everyone lift their right arm and point it at that hill over there."

Cujo tried lifting his arm, but the suit wouldn't comply.

"Uh," Ellen said. "I can't move."

"Same," Luna said.

"Yeah, what the hell?" Maze said.

Brax chuckled. "It learns from you, remember? It mimics and stores that data. Keep trying."

After about the sixth attempt, Cujo's right arm lifted and pointed directly at the hill, though it still took some effort.

"See," Brax said and clapped his hands together sharply. "Good. Now tell the suit this: Missiles."

Nearly in unison, Cujo's team repeated Brax.

A band of missiles emerged from the suit and encircled Cujo's forearm.

"Whoa," Benny said through some speaker inside Cujo's suit.

"For safety reasons, you will not deploy the missiles here," Brax said. "But remember, if you need to use them just say, "Fire, plus however many you wish to shoot at somethin'. Same with the laser. Say the word laser and the suit will deploy it. Want it to cut through somethin'? Say cut. That's it."

Brax waited a few heartbeats, then said, "Okay. Let's get to work on teaching the suits your movements."

It took until dusk for the team to train the suits to interact and mimic each one perfectly. And that was just on land, though the underwater training wasn't as bad as Cujo feared, either. Though, according to Brax, swimming in the shallows wasn't the same as the deep. But at least the suit would be acquainted with water and the intakes, or gills, would be ready. It was close to midnight by the time they finished, but everyone, though tired, loved the suits.

Brax told them all to get some sleep and made sure to look at every team member in turn when he spoke.

"We won't be here in the morning, but I'll maintain the link between us in case of issues." He smiled while his team loaded the suits on the large charter the Cryptid Force Six planned to use. "Don't expect an immediate response, though. Gonna be busy as shit and over two thousand miles away. So, don't get your shit in a twist, got me?"

Everyone shook hands, most of them too tired to say more than thank you before staggering off to the hotel.

Cujo and Brax followed behind.

"Ya know," Brax said after a moment. "When they told me I'd be working with Captain Arron "Cujo" Wright, I didn't believe 'em."

Cujo, barely able to keep his eyes open as they approached the hotel, said, "Oh?"

"Yup. Thought ya would've been retired by now. Livin' the life in Hawaii or somewhere."

"I hate the tropics," Cujo said.

"What?" Brax said and chuckled. "Who could hate all this?"

"Me." Cujo yawned. The hotel wasn't far now.

"Fair enough. Guess this is my way of sayin' I respect ya, Cap, and it was an honor working with you."

Cujo grunted. "Back at ya. Not quite how I remembered you from Afghanistan. That's why I was apprehensive at first."

"Dude, I was twenty-five and leading a brand-new team of monster hunters. I was an arrogant shit."

"Hell yeah, you were," Cujo said. "Still kinda are, just not as blatant."

Brax waved a dismissive hand. "Just a bit these days, man. Mostly just for show now." He shot Cujo a gentle smile. "It was an honor, Captain. I mean that with all my heart."

Cujo smiled back. "Honor is mine." He paused a second or two, and added, "I'm not a Captain for the US Military anymore, though. I'm the leader of the Cryptid Force Six." He snorted. "Just call me Cujo from now on."

"Done deal," Brax said.

They stopped at the hotel doors and Brax held out his hand. Cujo shook it and patted the man's shoulder.

"You're a good leader, Brax. Been hunting monsters longer than us and it was good to see how a more experienced team functions."

Brax laughed and shook his head. "Functions? Did you see them? They can barely walk on their own sometimes." Cujo couldn't help but laugh before Brax added, "We get the job done, man. That's all that matters. Might deviate from traditional military ranks and all that, but we're still a platoon. A team. That's all ya need to be. Oh, and always kick ass."

Brax turned and began walking away.

"You guys flyin' out tonight?" Cujo asked.

Brax didn't stop walking but glanced over his shoulder and said, "It'll only take a couple hours in my jet. Thinkin' early mornin'. Good luck, Cujo. Kick some ass."

Brax eventually disappeared into the deep shadows of the town. Where he was going, Cujo didn't know, but assumed the jet the man spoke of.

Cujo turned to the doors, opened one, and made his way to his room.

Tomorrow was going to be a hell of a day…

FIFTEEN

No one set their alarms.

Cujo woke at ten-thirty in the morning, the Baja sunlight blinding him from the room's window.

He shot out of bed and called his team.

"We overslept. Meet you all at the charter in fifteen minutes."

He was kicking himself for forgetting to set his alarm. Tired or not, he was the damn leader, after all. Out of them all, he should have been on task and prepared.

He showered, got dressed, grabbed his duffle bag of ammo and guns, and ran to the docks where their charter waited.

And Mary.

Cujo tossed his duffle bag onto the charter and turned to Mary. He was about to ask why she was there but his Spanish was too limited. Benny, Maze, and Wade rushed up the dock and hopped on the charter without a word. All of them appeared too pale. Too weary. Which worried Cujo a bit.

No sign of Luna or Ellen.

Mary smiled, said something in Spanish and got onto the charter boat.

Cujo sighed and followed suit. He really needed to know why she was there but without Ellen, he could only pick out a few words here and there. And that was only if Mary spoke slowly.

"Where the hell are Luna and Ellen?" Maze said. Her tone was louder than it needed to be.

Again, Cujo wasn't sure what was going on between Maze and Luna, but they had a job to do and all the drama was getting to be so stupid.

"Call Ellen," Cujo told Maze. "We're late as it is."

Maze frowned but brought out her phone. In a minute or so, she was yelling at the phone, calling Ellen a slut and liar, and everything in between.

"That's enough," Cujo boomed. "I don't care what's going on between you two. We have a mission to complete. Tell her to get Luna and get their asses on the charter. *Now*."

Maze blinked at Cujo and glanced at Benny, who shrugged.

She fidgeted a bit in her seat and said, "Just get Luna and hurry the fuck up." She hung up and refused to make eye contact with anyone.

Mary was trying to tell Cujo something, but he couldn't understand. Her expressions however, appeared dire. Tears welled in her eyes. She tugged on his arm and pulled a photo from the pocket of her shorts.

Cujo frowned at the photo. A shirtless man smiled at the camera behind a large grill. Cujo guessed he was in his early twenties. The photo itself was crumpled and torn in spots around the edges. Worn. So, a photo someone stuffed in their wallet for a couple of years, perhaps. The young man had shaggy black hair and the most brilliant white smile Cujo had ever seen.

"Hermano," Mary said. She repeated the word over and over. She slapped the side of the large fishing charter. "Hermano!"

"What's she freaking out about?" Benny asked.

"She's upset about the boat, maybe?" Maze said. She walked over to Mary and looked at the picture. "Who is it, do you think?" She looked at Cujo.

He shrugged. "Husband, maybe?"

"Why would she call the boat her husband?" Benny said.

Cujo rolled his eyes, "I doubt that's what she was saying. Cram it for now, okay?"

Benny shrugged and turned in his seat to look out over the vast, blue Pacific. The guy was like a brother to Cujo but acted like he was in high school half the time.

Mary gave up trying to tell him whatever she was so stressed about and plopped down on a seat. It was important, he realized, but with his limited Spanish and how quickly she spoke, he couldn't decipher any of it.

Cujo sighed, wiped sweat from his forehead and brought out a bottle of water. He drank about half and stowed it in the charter's full-sized fridge. The charter was a large eighty-footer. Built to accommodate the wealthier families, no doubt. Longer expeditions too, considering the fridge and stove. He wondered how much Gabino Garcia made a year? If his fishing charters drew tourists like authentic cuisines from various cultures thriving in Baja, then Cujo suspected Gabino was a very rich man, indeed.

By the time Ellen and Luna set foot on the dock, running toward the charter, it was almost nine in the morning. Cujo expected to be out by eight.

"Sorry," Ellen said while they boarded. "I must've shut my alarm off."

"Whore," Maze said.

"Same here," Luna said.

"Whore," Maze said.

Ellen started toward Maze. "What the fuck is your problem?"

Cujo caught her arm and pulled her back. He swung her around and pointed at Mary.

"Something is bothering her. Set the bullshit aside and get back to the mission."

Ellen yanked out of his grip and shot him a glare. "Talk to *her*, then. She's been treating me like shit the entire trip and I'm over it."

By her, Cujo assumed Ellen meant Maze.

"I'm not talking to anyone. You both figure your shit out after the mission. I want you on task. If you can't do that, go back to the hotel."

Everyone in the team blinked at him, though, eventually they all nodded too. He had strived not to make the team too militaristic in the beginning, but time had proven he'd been too damn lax. They were all acting like stupid teenagers. Especially lately. It was beyond time for him to whip them into some kind of shape.

They were all former military and, at least during missions, should act like it.

"I want all of you to listen to me, now," Cujo said and gestured for the charter captain to get moving. "We're out of our element. The ocean was never my thing." He nodded at Ellen. "Except for Ellen, we don't have much experience with water engagement."

He waited to see if Ellen, a former Navy SEAL, wanted to add anything. Instead, she sat next to Mary, and they chatted quietly. Mary showed Ellen the photo.

Cujo returned his attention to the rest of the team while the boat captain pulled away from the docks.

"We need to be on the same page once we're out there. And if we need to use the suits, we stay together. We're a team and I want us to be the best at what we do." He leveled his gaze on Benny. "That means when we're on, we're on. Vacation or not. We might not be in the military anymore, but that shouldn't matter during a mission. I expect the same discipline from you. I expect the same courage and passion. A dedication to saving lives." Cujo looked away from Benny and continued. "We stand for something, even if we don't serve officially anymore. We serve to protect the people. Not just in America, but every nation we find ourselves in. We are soldiers against the unknown. Defenders of what lurks in the dark." He paused, realizing he was making some kind of motivational speech. Something he had never done before. For a moment, he was at a loss for words. Finally, he straightened and added, "We kicked reanimated yeti asses. We beat devils. Now let's put an end to the Black Demon. All in, or nothing."

His team stared at him for a long time before Luna stood and snapped a salute. "Yes, Sir!"

Benny stood and saluted, "Yes, Boss."

Maze nodded and nodded. "Agreed, Pops." She saluted.

Wade was already standing and saluting the entire time. When Cujo looked at him, he nodded. "Semper Fi! Oo-Rah!"

Cujo stood tall. They might stray from the rules from time to time. They might be insubordinate. Considering they weren't bound by military rules, Cujo could forgive insubordination from time to time. Drama within the team, however, that's what irked him the most. An issue he watched grow larger and chose to stomp down a bit right now. Being friends was one thing, family, even, but when all that spills into work...that was a problem. There was a reason why he tried to not get too close to his platoons or the various teams he'd commanded. You get too close to people and the team loses sight of who is in control and flounders during times of high stress.

Benny stood, smiled, snapped a salute and sat back down.

Maze, though, she was frowning. A very deep frown. Her eyes fixed on Cujo and would not shift away. She didn't say anything, nor did she salute like the others.

He opened his mouth, about to ask her what was wrong when Ellen said, "It's her brother."

Cujo's mouth snapped shut. He turned to Ellen and Mary.

Ellen patted Mary's knee and stood. "She was showing you this picture because it's her brother on the missing charter. It's personal for her and she wanted us to leave yesterday." Ellen leveled her gaze on Cujo. "She wanted us to leave yesterday, and we ignored her calls..."

Cujo blinked. "What calls?"

"I guess she called the hotel several times but we weren't there and after a while, the concierge kept hanging up on her."

Cujo clenched his jaw, not sure how to respond.

Ellen moved closer to him. "She's terrified, Cujo. Something isn't right. Besides the obvious, something feels off with her."

"Like what?" He glanced at Mary.

Ellen shrugged. "I don't know. It's just a feeling. I might be wrong."

Cujo nodded. "Keep an eye on her. Make sure you both are staying hydrated too."

Ellen nodded, grabbed a couple of bottles of water from the refrigerator, and sat down beside Mary where they chatted quietly.

Cujo returned his attention to the rest of the team. "Put your throat mics on. I'm going to have Reece linked to us. She might have important intel while we're on the hunt for this thing."

No one said a word, not even Benny. They stood and rummaged through their duffle bags. He liked the efficiency and no nonsense, but at the same time it saddened him a bit. Like he just ripped the soul out of the team. They were proud and all in. But, even this early, he felt like something was missing. Something vital and unique to only his team.

No time to dwell on it now.

He found his own throat mic, secured it, and tucked the earbud in. He tapped the power button.

Static filled his right ear for a few minutes, then the familiar beep of the link being connected.

"Where the hell have you all been?" Reece shouted into Cujo's ear, startling him.

Not only him, but the team as well.

"Fuck," Benny spouted and pulled the earbud from his ear for a couple of seconds, cringing.

Cujo, ear still ringing, pressed his throat mic and said, "Settle down. What's wrong?"

"Don't tell me to settle down. I've been trying to reach you for an hour. Your boat is heading in the wrong direction. The charter we're pinging is south, you're going east!"

"Shit," Cujo said and darted up the few steps to the cramped wheelhouse. "Hey, man, why are we—"

The captain's chair was empty.

Cujo's eyes widened. His heart gave a hard knock against his ribs. He glanced around, thinking maybe the captain had wandered over to the narrow bathroom. But the door stood open and the toilet fully visible from where he stood. He hurried to the wheelhouse door and stepped out into the glaring sun and salty heat of a platform overlooking the twenty-foot deck where all the fishing was to be done in ordinary circumstances.

No sign of the captain on the deck either.

Cujo spun around, stepped back into the wheelhouse, and pressed his throat mic.

"Captain isn't here."

"What?" Reece said. "Where the hell did he go?"

"No idea. No sign of him in the wheelhouse or deck."

"Bathroom, maybe?"

"Nope. That's empty too." He stared at the wheel in front of a mounted swivel chair and a few levers near at hand. "We're on our own out here."

"Why would he leave?" Reece asked. "That doesn't make any sense."

Cujo sat in the captain's chair. "I dunno, but I need to know how to drive a boat like this."

"Um, I'm the monster expert, not the boat expert."

"Can you figure out a way to show me how to at least steer this thing? We're wasting time."

Reece paused. "Hold on. Getting in contact with the Devil Divers."

Cujo sighed. In the meantime, the large charter was barreling through the Pacific Ocean. A trap, but set by who? Cujo glanced at a lever. It had a rabbit at the top and a turtle on the bottom. Fast and slow. He grabbed the lever's horizontal handle and pulled back toward the turtle symbol.

He slammed forward into the wheel so hard the force shoved the wind out of him.

The boat slowed and Cujo about fell out of the chair, clutching his midsection like he just had a heart attack.

"Shit," he said through clenched teeth.

Groans floated up from below deck.

"The hell just happened?" Benny said, paused, and added, "Goddamn it. Water got on my sandwich."

The large boat rocked from side to side, rose and fell, creating massive vertigo. Cujo clutched the wheel so he didn't go tumbling onto the floor.

"Gah!" Benny said. "Boss! Wade just puked on my rucksack!"

Sounds of a few others vomiting also leaked their way to the wheelhouse.

Eyes closed, Cujo counted backward from ten until the vertigo passed. Eventually, he let go of the wheel and sat, gaping through reinforced glass at the Pacific Ocean. He took a few deep breaths to ease the stammering of his heart.

Somehow the old ticker just keeps tickin', his Grandpa would tell him from time to time when he was a kid.

Old...

Sixty wasn't considered old, but he definitely felt it these days. If he was still in his forties, the boat incident wouldn't have bothered him much. Just like it didn't seem to bother Benny much.

"Okay," Reece said through Cujo's earbud. "Brax says to ease the throttle slowly toward the turtle symbol."

Cujo sighed. "Too late."

"Oh," Reece said. "Okay. He also says there should be a compass, but if it's a charter, it might have GPS. Type in the coordinates and the vessel should steer itself in the general direction. Then you take over from there and keep the course."

Cujo glanced around. "Where the hell is the GPS?"

"Sorry. According to Brax, it should be directly in front of you. If not GPS, which he thinks it is, but if not, it will resemble a large compass."

Cujo frowned, glanced in front of him and rolled his eyes. "Well, shit. Yeah, it's GPS."

A long pause from Reece. "You know how to operate a GPS, right?"

Cujo sighed. "Yes. I'm old, but not *that* old."

Reece snickered and Cujo couldn't help but smile.

"Okay," Cujo said. "Over and out."

"Jesus, Pops," Maze said, stepping beside him on the left. "A little warning next time, huh?"

"The captain—"

"I know," she said. "We can all hear you when you're on the mic, remember? But maybe you could have waited a minute or two until our Good Doctor could respond with the correct information?"

"Or told us to hold on to something?" Luna said.

"Or brought some tequila," Benny said.

"Ugh," Wade said. "Don't even talk about alcohol right now."

"You puked on my sandwich, ya bastard."

"I couldn't fucking help it, man. I get motion sickness bad and—"

"Listen up," Cujo said, cutting the argument in two. For a wonder, they all fell silent. "We were set up. Someone paid the captain to abandon us. Maybe they even know we didn't know how to run a charter."

"You don't know that for sure, though," Ellen said.

"No." Cujo clenched his jaw and glared at the GPS. Finally, he nodded at it. "But look. We were aimed directly for Guadalupe Island."

The island itself was a couple hundred miles east yet, but it was obvious to Cujo the plan.

"Whoever knew we'd be on this charter wanted us to hit that island at full speed. Which would have probably killed us. The coordinates were purposely set on the GPS and..." He glanced around a bit until he found what he was looking for. A cruise control/ autopilot switch. He tapped it. "This." He flipped the autopilot switch off and the charter veered left. Cujo held onto the wheel and slowed the boat down to an idle.

"We were set up?" Benny said. "What the fuck? By who? Only people who know us are the Devil Divers, Reece and Ross, and..."

Cujo blinked. "Mary and her father..."

Cujo stood and glanced around. "Where is she?"

Ellen frowned. "She's resting. Told me she was getting too worked up and needed to sleep."

"*What*?" Maze said. "And you fucking let her?"

"I thought we trusted her." She faced Maze fully.

Both women stood firm for a good two minutes.

"Never trust anyone," Maze said.

"Well, you seemed to trust her just fine before, hun," Ellen said. "Otherwise, your ass wouldn't be here."

Maze moved closer to Ellen, fists clenched. "Don't ever call me hun. I swear to god I'll rip your throat out if you—"

"Enough," Cujo boomed, startling both women. "Whatever lover's quarrel you two got going on, stow it until the mission is over. Ellen, did you see Mary in a bunk?"

Ellen nodded. "Yes. She rolled up in my blanket."

Maze rolled her eyes and turned away from Ellen. "Let's see if she's still in the room and what she has on her. Tracking device, maybe?"

"She's not like that," Ellen said.

"How the fuck do you know?" Maze spun back around to Ellen. "You've known her for, what...a *day*? You don't know shit about her."

Ellen, back straight, fully turned to Cujo. "I'm going to check on Mary, if that's okay?"

Cujo nodded. "Go." He shot a glance at Wade. "You go too."

Ellen stopped walking mid-stride. "I don't need a chaperone, Cujo."

Cujo smiled. "I know. But, better safe than sorry. He goes with and I want you both to be careful. Something strange is going on here and Mary might know something. Even if she is innocent."

Ellen's lips pressed together in a firm, white line. She spun away and hurried down the steps to the lower deck of the charter. Wade followed after her.

Cujo sighed and looked at the rest of the team. "I want you all to stay vigilant. That includes putting personal issues aside." He shot a glare at Maze, who shook her head and looked away. He ignored the insubordination, as he had since the team assembled. They weren't in the military anymore. They didn't follow those rules, nor did they have to.

"We're here to find a stranded fishing charter, save who we can, and kill some big ass shark that's not supposed to exist. It's not only our mission, but we're getting paid for it. It's our job now. Stay focused. Don't hesitate." He glanced at each one in turn. "And let's kick this shark's ass."

His team, minus two, stood straight and still. None of them said anything. They didn't need to. All, even Maze and Benny, stood at attention. They didn't salute. They didn't need to. He saw the warrior in every set of eyes his connected with. He saw a team finally knitting together for the first time. There would be more stumbles, of course, but right here and now...they got it. They knew the stakes. They knew who to trust. They were ready to kill monsters and save lives.

It was the same sets of eyes looking back at him as his platoon before they deployed to Afghanistan.

"We need to find out who is behind sabotaging our boat," Cujo said and sat in the captain's chair. "That's our third operation. We focus on saving lives first, but don't let your guard down. We need to find out who just tried to kill us."

All three nodded.

Maze opened her mouth, then closed it again.

"What?" Cujo said.

Maze looked him directly in the eyes. "I don't trust Mary."

"Well, if there's anything strange about her, we'll find out shortly."

She nodded and glanced toward the narrow stairwell to the lower deck. He followed her gaze then returned it to her.

"Maze," he said, as tenderly as possible.

She blinked and looked at him.

"It will be okay."

Cujo held her gaze longer than he thought he would before she turned and walked away. She got the message. At least he hoped she did.

God, he thought, *I'm getting too soft.*

Or, more like he'd learned how to integrate emotion into his leadership over the years. Albeit in slivers.

Mary emerged from the stairwell with Ellen and Wade in tow.

"She was sleeping," Ellen said. "She says she doesn't know why the captain left. He's one of her father's most trusted charter captains."

"Uh-huh," Maze said and spun around. "So, her dad gave us his best captain for the mission. A captain who fucking, *literally*, jumped ship. Looks like her father set us up."

"Or," Ellen said, stepping in front of Mary, "the captain was paid off by someone else."

Maze snorted. "Right. The likeliness of that is like seeing a unicorn dry hump a goddamn griffin."

"Look—"

Cujo, hands clasped behind his back, stepped between the two women, halting Ellen's retort.

Maze glared at him in her usual defiance, though amped up to ten. He hadn't seen that expression since the day they teamed up, when she thought she should be the leader and Cujo was too old. Hell, there were times now he wondered if she was right back then. Maybe he was too old for this shit. Regardless, he wouldn't step down until forced to do so. Maybe then, Maze would get her chance to lead.

Maybe...

"This bickering," Cujo said, "isn't doing us any good. You're both speculating and wasting time." He glanced over his shoulder at Ellen. She sighed. He returned his gaze to Maze. Her defiant expression weakened a bit. "We finish the mission we were sent to do. When we get back to land, our new mission will be to track down the reason for the captain leaving."

"How'd he even do it, though?" Benny asked. "Did he really just jump off the boat and expect to swim back to shore?"

"Inflatable raft or small schooner is my guess," Wade said.

"Right," Benny said. "But we were going a gazillion miles per hour, or whatever that is in boat speak. Wouldn't it be damn near impossible to drop a boat or raft into the water with us moving so fast?"

Cujo nodded. "So, he must have set a course and speed and left without us seeing him."

"At the docks," Luna said.

"Yup."

"That motherfucker," Benny said and kicked one of the mounted chairs. "Shit! Ouch." He limped away toward one of the windows on the opposite side of the captain's chair.

Cujo rolled his eyes and glanced at his team. "This is where we're at. We find the fishing charter. We kill the Black Demon. Then we go kick the ass of whoever fucked with us."

Silence spread throughout the wheelhouse.

Then Wade said, "Oo-rah."

The rest of the team looked at him, even Benny turned, then gave Cujo their full attention.

No one else said oo-rah, but they didn't have to. The look in their eyes was enough, like earlier, to convince him. They were getting dialed in and focusing on the mission at hand. Finally...

"Now," Cujo said and sat in the captain's chair. "Let's kill us a cryptid shark."

He turned the boat south.

Reece told him the coordinates for the missing charter and he typed them in. So, the boat set course for the southeast of Baja. Over one thousand miles of open water, except for a few small islands here and there.

He thought about the captain abandoning the ship.

He thought about his team.

And, as they neared the location, he wondered if this massive shark even really existed, or if it was a ploy to find Mary's brother, or simply kill them all in some hideous fashion.

He didn't know. But one thing was for sure...

He hated mysteries.

SIXTEEN

They reached Reece's coordinates within three hours.

It was a little after noon and hotter than a bonfire in Hell. Cujo cracked open a water, screwed off the cap and downed half of the bottle.

He wiped sweat from his face with a hand towel he found in the kitchen area below deck and returned to the wheelhouse where his team waited.

"Uh," Benny said. "There's supposed to be a boat here?"

"It's just...gone," Reece said through their earbuds. "I don't know where it went."

"When did it disappear?" Cujo asked through his throat mic, while slowing the boat and killing the engine. "I didn't see anything as we approached."

"It just popped back up again," Reece said. "See anything?"

Cujo glanced out the windshield. Nothing but rolling water in all its vast, blue glory. He pressed the throat mic and switched to constant stream so they could talk freely.

"Reece, are you sure your equipment isn't glitching? There's nothing here."

"The equipment is top notch, Cujo. Something is there, but..." She paused.

"What?"

"But it might be underwater."

Cujo's heart ached a bit. Not the words he wanted to hear.

"So," Maze said. "The charter sank?"

"Appears so," Reece said. "You guys will have to try out those new diving suits sooner than you thought."

Maze grunted and crossed her arms over her chest. "Yeah."

A shiver worked its way over Cujo's sweaty skin. He didn't want to get back in that thing even if his claustrophobia wasn't triggered much. There was still the knowledge of being trapped in the suit in the Pacific Ocean with whatever lurked in the cold, dark waters below.

"My guess," Reece said, severing his thoughts, "is it hasn't sunk to the bottom. That's how I keep pinging it so clearly. It's bobbing up and down. Like now, it just disappeared again."

"What the hell could be keeping it afloat like that, though?" Benny asked.

"I'm not sure. Air trapped in the hull, perhaps?" Reece paused for a few seconds. "That's it."

Cujo frowned. "What?"

"Cujo, if there are survivors, they'd be in the hull where there's air."

His gaze drifted to the sparkling, rolling blue ocean outside the wheelhouse.

"That seems like a dumb choice, though," Maze said. "Why lock yourself in the hull while you're sinking? You'd die anyway, eventually."

The wheelhouse fell silent for a bit.

"Preferences," Ellen said.

Cujo blinked and everyone looked at Ellen.

"Huh?" Benny said.

Ellen took a deep breath and blew it out. Instead of addressing Benny, she turned to Cujo, sullen. "Preferences. They'd rather suffocate or drown than face whatever was in the water waiting for them."

Cujo drew in a slow breath and another shiver slithered through him. He knew what Ellen was talking about. Saw it plenty in Afghanistan. People so afraid of the Taliban, they huddled in rubble rather than be shot, or worse, taken prisoner and tortured. Beheaded...

Often, fear shoved rational thought to the backseat and took the wheel only to, sooner or later, run ninety miles per hour into a tree. Sometimes, people would rather die on their own terms than by someone else...or something else.

Cujo exhaled and stood from the captain's chair. "We're dropping anchor here. Let's save some lives."

No one said a thing and hurried out of the wheelhouse and onto the deck where the diving suits were kept. Cujo eventually found the anchor release button and pushed it.

"You can't anchor here," Reece said. "The anchor of this particular charter only goes to approximately three hundred feet, or ninety-one meters. According to the Pacific Ocean depth map, which is iffy because it's difficult to accurately measure depths in the ocean, you're about one thousand feet deep."

"Oh, lovely," Cujo said and pressed the anchor up button. "So...we just drift? What if we surface and the boat is gone?"

"You need to have someone on the surface to keep the boat in the general area. Plus, your suits can locate their own docks."

"Reece, I'm the only one of the team who even kind of knows how to drive this damn thing."

"Mary," Reece said. "She's the owner's daughter. I bet she knows how to at least keep a charter boat from drifting away from a certain spot."

Cujo blinked, kicking himself for not thinking of the idea first. It was so damn obvious. Even though there were some trust issues. Still, without Reece, the team would flail. Hell, everyone would probably be dead by now. She was their secret seventh member. The scientist. The cryptid expert.

"Thanks," he said and switched the throat mic feed from community to individual.

Ellen stood behind him with Mary at her side when he turned around.

"I told her, and she said she'd keep the charter as still as possible for our return," Ellen said.

Cujo's gaze held Ellen's. "And you, without a doubt, know we can trust her?"

Ellen nodded. "Yes, sir."

His gaze drifted from Ellen to Mary and back again. "I want you to stay with her for the extraction."

Ellen frowned and cocked her head to the side slightly. "You don't trust her either."

"Until I know for sure who set us up, no. Keep her company and keep your eyes and ears peeled for anything strange."

She nodded and Cujo hurried to the deck and the diving suit he loathed just thinking about. Still, a mission was a mission. *Suck it up and get it done, old man,* he thought and joined the rest of the team.

The suit opened like before and he backed into it. The thing entombed him before he had a chance to draw in a breath. He stood in utter darkness long enough to wonder if he was really trapped inside the thing. Long enough for his heart to quicken and his bowels to churn. Then the helmet screen opened. The gauges and commands flickered on. The suit began to hiss as it sealed him inside.

He took a few slow breaths, allowing his heart to ease a bit.

In his ear, Reece said, "Brax gave me the code to patch into the suits' communication system. Once you all are online, I'll get that set up."

Cujo closed his eyes, ignoring the tiny beads of sweat trickling down his forehead. A series of beeps sent his easing heart into rapid mode again.

"There," Reece said. "Can you all hear me?"

Everyone mumbled an offhanded, "Yeah."

Cujo closed his eyes and breathed. Why was it so difficult this time than before?

"Cujo?" Reece, on the edge of concern. "Are you okay?"

Cujo breathed. He kept his eyes closed. He focused on slowing his heart rate. Wade was also claustrophobic, but the guy seemed perfectly fine in the suit. No complaints yet, anyway.

So, what's my deal? he asked himself.

"Boss?" Benny said.

"Pops, you good?" Maze said.

A few seconds crawled by, and he managed, "Yeah."

"You sure?" Luna asked.

He released a shaky sigh. "Y-Yeah. Just getting used to this thing again."

"Cujo," Reece said. "Brax mentioned if you exhibited any problems in the suit that you should lead from the surface. Otherwise, you're a liability and danger to the team."

He gritted his teeth. Brax had too much influence on his team and he wasn't sure how to take that until it sank in a bit. Brax was not only looking out for him, but the team. Cujo had to keep reminding himself…Brax wasn't the bad guy, despite the man's abrasive nature. If Cujo was freaking out in the suit, he couldn't effectively lead. And, especially in the ocean, there couldn't be any fuck ups.

Regardless, his nerves eased, and his heart settled to its usual rhythm where he didn't notice it anymore. He blew out a breath, inhaled, and said, "I'm good. Just had a moment there."

"You sure, Pops?" Maze said.

"Yeah. Let's see about getting those people out."

The team walked to the side of the boat.

"You'll want to go in off the left side of the boat," Reece said. "Whatever that is in boat talk."

They were on the right side and moved to the left.

"How deep?" Cujo asked.

"I don't know. About thirty meters is my guess. But it's bobbing up and down, so the depths are unknown for now."

Cujo sighed and looked at the rolling blue water about twenty feet from the boat's deck. The large charter boat rose and fell in the rolling ocean and the suit adjusted to the motion, learning from his subtle movements to keep him balanced.

"Cryptid Force," Cujo said. "Ready to save some lives?"

"Hell yeah," everyone said in near unison.

Cujo drew in a breath and leaped into the water.

SEVENTEEN

A wall of bubbles cleared, giving way to, at first, nothing but a vast dark blue abyss.

UPSIDE DOWN, appeared on the right side of his helmet visor, followed by, DIVE?

Cujo shook his head, realizing he was, indeed, staring into an abyss. Beautiful and terrifying. An endless descent into oblivion. No wonder oceans fascinated people so much. It was the ultimate mystery. What lurked down there?

What could be watching...waiting...

He shifted his body, using his arms and legs to get him to float upright.

"Oxygen intakes engaged," a gentle voice said, one he'd heard before a couple of times during their brief training. "Stabilizing."

"Guys," Maze said. "This is weird."

"Didn't Brax say not to look down?" Benny said.

"No, idiot," Wade said. "He said to imagine the sand not far from our feet."

"Let's just get these people to safety," Luna spouted. "I'm tired of the bickering."

Cujo nodded. "Luna is right. Find the charter and rescue the survivors."

"Stay where you are," Reece said. "It should be ascending in about five seconds."

Not wanting to, but unable to help himself, Cujo looked down and the abyss stared back. Deep blue eventually succumbed to complete darkness. He shivered and looked to the surface. Daylight shimmered through the rolling water.

He was in a different world now. One that hadn't been fully explored. One he wasn't sure he would survive and—

"There," Maze said.

"Jesus," Benny said. "It's like a fucking ghost, man."

Cujo looked down in time to see a white object emerging from the dark depths. His heart stuttered upon seeing it and, yes, it made him think of a ghost. Something eerily white shrouded in gloom.

Soon enough, however, the bow of a charter boat became visible. He took a couple of slow breaths, letting his heart calm down.

"Wait for it to get closer to the surface," Cujo said. "We don't want to drown the people we're trying to rescue."

No one said anything and suddenly Cujo got the strange feeling like he was being watched. The same feeling you might get when someone is staring at you from behind or the side. A sense of unease...

He looked to his left but found only one of his team in their dive suits. He wasn't sure who. The ocean beyond appeared void of life. To his right, the rest of his team waited for the boat to ascend closer to the surface. The rest of the ocean was nothing but a dark blue canvas. He almost turned around, but the boat approached quicker than he expected.

"We're not going to have enough time," Luna said. "I think it's coming up too—"

"Look out," Maze shouted.

Cujo flailed away from the area the boat would ascend through, barely escaping being struck by the thing.

"Fuck," Benny said. "I didn't know boats could do that with a little air in them."

"Me either," Wade said.

"Reece?" Cujo said while he stabilized himself. "Copy?"

"Yes."

"Do you know if sunken boats behave like this one? With air in the hull, can it really rise and fall so fast?"

"Hey, Cap," Brax blasted through the suit's speakers. "How's it hangin'? Little to the left?"

Cujo rolled his eyes. "You heard the questions. We need the answers."

"Yeesh, settle your ass down, Cap. I mean, I'm here to help, ya know?"

"I fucking know," Cujo shouted. "We need intel on how a charter boat, hull partially filled with air, will behave."

"Easy-peasy, my man," Brax said. "Is the propeller still rotating?"

Cujo frowned and glanced upward as the charter bobbed on the surface. A chaos of bubbles and churning water confirmed everything.

"Looks like it," Cujo said.

"That's your answer, then," Brax said. He paused for a few seconds. "Hold on, got this big bastard to take care of."

Silence stretched out for at least a minute before Maze said, "So...should we rescue those people, Pops, or just let them go for another deep-sea dunking?"

"Let's go," Cujo said, figuring it didn't really matter why the charter was bobbing up and down like it was. "Use the lasers to cut through the hull but aim high. Just in case."

"High boost," Cujo told his suit. "Six feet below the surface."

A tiny beep and he was thrusted toward the surface, though not directly for the boat. He flailed his arms, trying to keep near the charter boat, but was instead flung away from it.

Brax wasn't kidding when he said high boost is high boost. Zero to sixty in three seconds. He cartwheeled a bit until the suit stabilized itself. Then he blinked at how far away he'd floated from the boat.

"How the hell...?"

"Boss?" Benny said. "Where'd you go? We're at the boat. It's already starting to go back down."

"I don't know what happened, but I'm about twenty feet away. Start cutting, I'm on my—"

"LARGE LIFEFORM DETECTED," the suit said. "REAR."

Cujo sucked in a sharp breath.

"Want to see?" the suit asked in a gentle tone completely opposite of the warning.

For a second or two he almost said no, but curiosity got the better of him.

"Yes."

The helmet's visor flickered. His view of the boat and team disappeared, giving way to the view behind him.

Eventually, he blew out a breath he didn't know he'd been holding.

The view behind him was only the open ocean. Maybe a small fish darted by, triggering the sensors of the suit or—

Everything went from blue to black in an instant. He sucked in a sharp breath, heart stumbling over itself.

"Pops?" Maze said. "Everything good?"

He opened his mouth to reply, but only a tiny squeak came out.

"Pops?"

The black slid away and all the strength in him loosened. What the hell was that? What—

"Boss," Benny shouted. "The fuck is—"

"There's something here with us," Cujo managed before terror took over him.

"*What?*" Maze said. "You see something?"

Cujo opened his mouth and closed it again. He needed to tell them about the darkness behind him but couldn't find his voice. No matter how much he tried.

Knock it off, he thought. *You've been through thousands of scary scenarios. This isn't any different.*

Except...it was.

In those other scenarios, he, in the very least, knew what his enemy was capable of. In the ocean, all he knew about the enemies were how big they could get and how many teeth they had. Did a shark think? Could it be cunning, or vengeful? Did orcas plan attacks? The more he thought about the latter, the more he shivered. He'd watched some documentary about orcas years ago. How they worked together to flip a seal off a small iceberg by creating large waves to rock the chunk of ice just enough…

"Boss? What the hell are you talking about? I don't see anything."

"Pops," Maze said. "You need to get your ass back over here."

"F-Forward boost, medium," he managed through numb lips. He'd never felt this kind of fear before and he hated it. Not even the parasitic yetis or hundreds of Jersey Devils struck this much fear in him. Like a cold spike plunged into his stomach.

He moved closer to the boat, watching its descent while the team worked at freeing the people inside.

"Come on, come on," Cujo whispered. Frustration cut through the fear a bit. It didn't even seem like he was halfway there yet. Where was the massive creature now? Was it watching him? Hunting him? Could it be opening its massive jaws this very second to chomp him in half?

But before he could tell the suit to increase its speed, he made it to the boat.

"Stop," he told the suit and he drifted to a stop beside one of his team, though he wasn't sure which one until they looked at him.

Benny winked. "Hey, Boss. Glad you could make it."

"Why don't we have these people out yet?" Cujo said.

"Because you said there was something here with us," Luna said.

"We were scanning for large lifeforms, but didn't find anything near us," Maze said.

Meanwhile, the boat continued to sink.

"Guess I was mistaken. Let's get 'em out and jet to the surface. Don't dawdle, either. Once we cut through, the hull will completely flood. We have less than a minute to get them topside."

"Got it," Benny said. "We ready?"

"On three, cut in, grab whoever you can and go," Cujo said. He pointed his left arm at the white hull. "One. Two. Three."

They sliced through the bow. Bubbles blasted into Cujo's face, obscuring his vision longer than he guessed and—

Something darted out of the bubbles and smacked directly into him.

"Human lifeforms detected," his suit informed him. Not the blaring warning voice, but the calm one.

It took him a couple of seconds to realize the thing hitting him was a man. Cujo went to take the man's arm, but the guy swam away.

"Goddamn it," Cujo muttered and swam after him.

Luna, Benny, and Wade all jetted to the surface, which left Cujo and Maze alone.

Cujo swam for the man, who now struggled about thirty feet above him, toward the surface. He flagged horribly, though. Didn't have much more time...

"Surface, fas—"

A massive black figure cut through the water and huge jaws snapped down over the man. The black figure became a wall for almost a minute, ending with the wide swoosh of its tail, which pushed him backward a bit until the suit stabilized. A small cloud of blood floated in the water like a scarlet ghost.

"Holy...*fuck*..." Maze said. "What was *that*?"

"Why aren't you people talking to me?" Reece said. "I'm hearing everything, but not getting any details. Brax is offline. What are you seeing?"

Cujo's mouth opened but all that came out was a thin whine.

"Hello?" Reece said.

"I..." Maze said but fell silent again.

Cujo cleared his throat and frowned at the cloud of blood, which had all but faded to nothing.

"I think...I think we found our cryptid shark."

"You saw it? The Black Demon?"

"Easy, girl," Maze said. "Don't get those undies wet."

"Yeah," Cujo said, looking around and finding, once more, nothing but the endless blue of the Pacific Ocean.

"I'm comin' back down, Boss," Benny said. "Let's get this bastard."

"No," Cujo said. "We need a better plan."

"He's right, Benny," Reece said. "There are dozens of reports saying the Black Demon isn't like any other shark. It hunts, sure, but it also seems to strategize, making it unpredictable."

"Well, that's just lovely," Benny said. "You two just gonna float around down there all day or are you going to join us so we can make a plan to kill this thing?"

Maze drifted close to Cujo. He looked at her.

"Ready?"

She nodded and looked to the surface.

"Surface," he told his suit. "High boost."

EIGHTEEN

"How the hell are we supposed to plan to kill a monster people never see coming?" Benny asked a few minutes after Maze and Cujo stepped out of their Devil 1 suits.

Cujo grabbed a water out of the fridge and sat at a modest dining table. He twisted the cap off and downed about half of the bottle and looked at Benny.

"And there's the rub, right?"

Benny nodded.

The rest of the team joined them in the kitchen/ dining area.

Maze shot a glare at Ellen and Mary when they entered. "Isn't she supposed to be making sure we don't fucking crash into something?"

Ellen rolled her eyes, leaned close to Mary, and whispered something into the woman's ear. Mary's dark eyebrows knitted together in a frown. Finally, she nodded and walked away toward the stairs to the wheelhouse.

"Where are the survivors?" Cujo asked.

"Resting in our rooms. They have water and food too."

Cujo looked away. "Good. I want to talk to them after we figure out a rough plan. Reece? Are you with us?"

"Dude," Benny said. "She's not a ghost."

Cujo rolled his eyes. "Reece? You there?" He looked at Benny. "Better?"

"Atta', Boss."

"You two are so weird," Reece said. She cleared her throat, and added, "Okay. I didn't find any reports on just how smart the Black Demon is, but I did find a more detailed report of a swordfish vessel being chased farther out to sea than the captain liked before it disappeared. They didn't have enough fuel to make it back to land and radioed for help. According to the captain's recordings, they were adrift for four days. They were out of food and about out of water. His crew of fifteen were too scared to take the small schooner or runner rafts and find land. They all wondered if the huge shark was still out there. The captain had his doubts, though. In one of his logs he wrote: "Sharks don't keep coming after prey they can't catch. They give up and move on to an easier meal. No matter how big it is, I know it moved on by now."

Reece paused. "Sorry, I'm pulling up more data from that event. Bear with me."

"I mean," Maze said. "Sure. Not like we have anywhere else to go."

"On the fifth day," Reece said, "according to the captain, not long after their water ran out and no help had shown up yet, something struck the bottom of the vessel hard enough to knock them all off their feet. A very large, black dorsal fin soon circled the vessel." Reece paused. "That's the last log the captain wrote."

No one said anything for a few seconds.

"So," Benny said. "This thing intentionally tortured the crew? Like it...enjoyed it?"

"It appears so," Reece said. "It waited days before finally finishing them off. All except for the captain."

"Oh, that's just fucking fantastic," Benny said. He started pacing. "We're so fucked, guys. We—"

"Shut up, Benny," Cujo said. He eyed the younger man. "Keep it together."

Benny gritted his teeth and spun away from Cujo, running both hands through his hair. He took a couple of deep breaths, nodded and faced Cujo.

"Sorry, Boss. This is all just...nuts."

Cujo smiled. "I'm scared too."

"What the..." Benny said. "I—I'm not scared, man. I just—" He waved a hand. "I never liked the ocean, anyway."

"Neither do I," Cujo said. "But we have a job to do and need to get it done."

"Yeah, man," Benny said. "I know. I know."

"Sorry to burst this little male bonding moment," Maze said, "but there's an evil shark out there that needs killing and we're not getting anywhere chatting about our feelings."

"Touché," Cujo said and turned his attention to the rest of the team. "So, we know the monster is smart enough to keep a boat adrift for days to starve a crew enough to weaken them."

"Tortured," Benny said. "You mean tortured them."

"Sure," Cujo said. "Tortured. Anyway, the fucking thing is smart, and we need to be smarter. I think we might need to trap it somehow."

"If you're talking about a net," Reece said, "won't work. Three reports of people trying to net the thing and it pulled the boats down with it."

Cujo sighed. "A net was one possibility, but I was thinking more of an ambush."

Everyone fell silent for a minute or two.

"How would you even ambush that thing?" Luna asked.

Cujo glanced at her then looked away. He shrugged and wiped sweat from his face with a nearby hand towel.

"I don't know. But Reece might."

"It might be smarter than other sharks, but I think it does have the same major weakness."

"What?" Cujo said.

"It can't swim backward, for one."

"Okay?" Benny said. "How's that a weakness that can help us?"

"There is no proof with the Black Demon, but it is a shark and sharks simply cannot swim backward. If pulled backward by the tail, it will die."

Cujo nodded. "So, we get a chain or something." He stood, heart thudding. "Right? Get a chain, or a harpoon. Snag the tail, hook the chain or whatever to the boat and full speed ahead."

Everyone looked at him, though no one disagreed.

"That just might work," Reece said. "If it can move its tail in the beginning, though, before the boat has time to move, you might have issues. Like with the nets, it might overpower the boat's motors and take you all down."

Cujo scratched his right cheek, thinking.

"So...we break it," Wade said.

"Yes, if you can do that," Reece said, "there would be no reason to drag it backward. If it can't move at all, it will die."

"So, take out the tail and we're golden," Maze said.

"Sounds that way," Cujo said, kicking himself for not realizing the obvious. Maybe he did and with all the stress, it just didn't blip on his radar very well. He'd noticed this happening more and more lately. Just old age or...?

He shook his head and said, "I want to find a way to trick it into cornering itself. Reece, how deep are we?"

A couple of seconds went by.

"You're drifting over one thousand feet to three hundred. Appears there might be sandbar, or a shelf of rock in that area."

Cujo nodded. "What's it look like around us, from what you can tell?"

A minute or so passed. "You mean below?"

"Yes. Are there any drop offs or cliffs? Things like that?"

"The boat should have a depth finder," Reece said.

"Probably," Cujo said, "but I want more details than that. I want to know exactly how the ocean floor looks."

"Okay. Hold on."

Ellen sighed. "I'm going to go check on Mary."

"Give her a kiss for me too," Maze spouted.

Ellen glared at Maze. Eventually, she looked away and said, "To make sure she's okay and we're not being compromised." Nothing derogatory. Blunt.

Ellen walked away before Maze could respond. Maze blinked, sighed and turned to Cujo.

"Why do we need to know what the ocean floor looks like if we're going to blow the damn thing's tail off?"

"Because it might not be that easy," Cujo said.

"How do you know? Maybe the shark is smart, but it's still a shark, right?"

"Right."

"Wrong," Reece said through the boat's speakers. "It is a shark with spliced gene pools, correct. Between a megalodon and what some believe to be an actual demon. And, if those accounts and reports are right, we're dealing with something almost supernatural here. Which would explain its intelligence and love of torture."

Nodding, Cujo said, "Sounds about right."

"It does?" Benny said and chuckled. "A fucking megalodon and an *actual* demon got it on thousands of years ago and made that thing? C'mon, Reece, I thought you were a scientist?"

"From the data I have collected so far, and granted, I am not as familiar with the Black Demon as I am with other cryptids, nothing is off the table. Supernatural, or not. Do I believe it's half demon, half megalodon? No, but I won't discard the idea entirely."

Benny snorted, shook his head and walked toward the stairs to the wheelhouse. He stopped and looked at the ceiling. "So, basically you don't know shit. Is that what I'm hearing?"

"*Benny*," Cujo said. He stood. "What the hell—"

Benny held up his hands. "Whoa, Boss, I meant about this particular cryptid. Sorry, Reece."

Reece didn't respond for about a minute.

"Hello? I think I lost you guys for a bit. Benny, if you responded, I didn't hear it. Can you repeat it, please?"

Cujo smiled. He knew sarcasm when he heard it. Reece heard everything.

Benny didn't appear to catch on.

"Uh, I said, well shit. Better get our proton packs on then, eh?" He snorted at his own wit, which wasn't really that witty.

"I don't know shit about the Black Demon, I don't think a fictional ghost catching device is going to help here."

Cujo lowered his head, chuckling to himself. A couple of the team members snickered.

Benny frowned. "I…um…wait, did you just—"

"Cujo, I have the images you need for the ocean floor directly below you right now and in a twenty-mile radius. I'm also catching brief blips of something large about five hundred feet deep and about a mile away. Appears to be getting closer."

Cujo glanced at Benny, then looked at one of the speakers in the ceiling.

"How close is it now?"

"Half a mile," Reece said. "But there is a ten second lapse."

"So," Cujo said, "it could be closer than that right now." Not a question. "Okay, kids, suit up. Reece, can you send the images to our suits somehow?"

"I can. Will be uploaded to all your dive suits now."

"Good," Cujo said. He glanced at his team, minus Ellen. "Let's do this." He stopped Maze. "Tell Ellen to stand guard here. Mary is probably innocent, but I want someone here to make sure shit doesn't hit the fan. Get to the deck once you relay the information. No drama."

Maze sighed, nodded, and hurried up the steps to the wheelhouse.

Cujo stared at the narrow set of stairs for a moment, then glanced in the direction where the survivors rested. He hurried down the hall to the first room and opened the door a crack. A man, maybe about the same age as Cujo, snored away on the bed. Cujo closed the door and checked the other three, who appeared younger than the man in Cujo's room. All were soundly asleep.

He started with the older man.

The man was a grizzled thing. A snarled mane of gray hair and scraggly gray beard. He was thin, to the point of scrawny, but Cujo noted the ropes of muscles that made up his exposed arms. The man might appear weak, but there was no doubt in Cujo's mind. The man was a tough one. He had seen such folks throughout the years. Scrawny. Thin. No bulking muscles. People saw them as weak. Not the case every time. He knew plenty of privates who could beat down the most muscular, or strongest soldier in the platoon.

Benny was one of them. Wiry bastard.

Cujo placed a hand on the snoring man's exposed shoulder and shook gently. The man snorted but didn't wake. Cujo shook harder. Still, the man didn't wake up. He was about to shake the man again—

"Hey, Boss," Benny whispered from the doorway. "We're ready to fuck us up a cryptid shark from hell. You—" He frowned and nodded at the man in bed. "He okay?"

Cujo shrugged and motioned for Benny to back up. Cujo stepped out of the room and closed the door.

"He's down for the count," Cujo said. "Probably for hours."

"Well, they were in the boat for a couple days, not sleeping and scared to hell, right?" Benny started walking away. "I'd be snoring my ass off too."

"Yeah," Cujo said and glanced over his shoulder at the closed door.

Something felt off about all this. Like tiny shards gradually coming together to form a whole piece. Something...

"Forty meters down, a little over a mile away and closing in fast," Reece said, startling Cujo. "If you guys are going to do something, I suggest you do it now."

Without further hesitation, Cujo and Benny sprinted for the deck and their dive suits.

NINETEEN

The team suited up and jumped into the water.

Cujo's heart slammed in his throat while Reece's images of the ocean floor scrolled across his visor. A red dot was where the charter boat drifted. Everything else was the ocean in a radius of twenty miles but nothing was very significant besides a sharp drop off approximately four miles north.

Something big cut through the water in front of him. He flailed, breath snagging in his throat like a rusty hook.

Across his helmet visor were the words: GREAT WHITE SHARK DETECTED.

"Shit," he muttered, trying to control the terror exploding through him. It didn't matter if the suit could withstand a great white bite or not, it was just the sheer terror of knowing one was actually around.

"GREAT WHITE SHARK DETECTED," the suit said. "FIFTEEN METERS SOUTH."

Cujo breathed a little easier and returned his focus on the ocean floor. Four miles north was the sharp drop-off. And holy shit it was indeed a drop-off. From almost one thousand feet to last known recorded depth, 4,000 feet and below. Cujo wondered if they might be somewhere near the Mariana Trench. Nothing was labeled, so he wasn't sure. This trench, however, did go on for what appeared to be forever. So, maybe it was the Mariana Trench after all.

"You all see that drop off, right?" he said.

"Yeah, Pops. Is that where this shindig is supposed to go down?"

"Looks like our best option."

"So do we just swim around until this thing shows up?" Luna said. "Or—"

Light beeping filled Cujo's helmet, then, "LARGE LIFEFORM APPROACHING."

"Looks like we won't have to," Cujo said.

"Goddamn it, Luna, and your shark whispering superpowers," Benny said.

Someone chuckled. Maybe Luna. Didn't matter.

"Reece, you copy?" Cujo said.

"Yep. It's coming in fast from the southwest. I lost it earlier then your area was clear, but it's back." She paused. "And guys…it's huge. Larger than I thought."

"Oh, well, isn't that just fuckin' lovely," Benny said.

"Luna, Wade, and Benny, I want you at the trench standing by," Cujo said.

"Maze, you and I are going to lead the thing around, get to the trench and deep dive forty meters down from current depth, and get this thing to smash itself into the rock cliff of the trench. Then we all take out its tail."

"Sounds like some crazy shit, Boss. Hope it works."

"I hope so too. Now get into position."

Two of his team shot off toward the trench while Maze floated closer to him. He could just barely see her eyes through the visor.

"How are we going to do this, Pops? Like, do you have a plan you weren't sharing with the rest of us or...?"

Cujo smiled. "Looks like we're winging it."

"Ugh. I knew you were gonna say that."

"Just don't get eaten," Cujo said.

"That's the best advice you can give me?"

Cujo snorted. "Don't die. That better?"

Maze was silent for a few seconds and sighed. "Yeah. Don't die."

They turned to the southwest and waited for hell to follow.

TWENTY

"It stopped," Reece said. "Sixty meters directly in front of you. I have never seen a shark just stop before. They need to keep moving to live, unless I'm missing something."

Cujo frowned at the deep, dark blue in front of him. "Sixty meters."

"Now it's veering to the east slowly," Reece said. "Maybe it senses you."

"Shit," Maze said. "Now what?"

Cujo sighed, not sure how to respond until Wade said, "We need bait."

"Bait," Cujo said. A flicker of an idea appeared in his mind.

"Twenty meters and closing," Reece said. "Slower now."

"We need blood," Cujo said. "Don't sharks go in a frenzy if there's blood in the water?"

"I guess?" Maze said.

"Not like in the movies," Reece said. "But it definitely attracts them, and they will attack anything in the area, according to some quick data here."

"So, we need blood?" Maze asked.

"Yes," Cujo said, looking up. "If you can catch a fish, or..." He frowned at all the scarlet water above them. "Why is there blood in the water?"

No one said anything for a bit.

"The charter boat is about thirty feet away from you," Reece said. "Unless another, smaller shark was feeding nearby..."

Cujo's heart whip-cracked. He glanced around but didn't see anything unusual besides the spreading cloud of blood.

"I don't see anything around and the suit isn't detecting anything," Cujo said.

"Where's all that blood coming fr—oh my god!"

Cujo turned, suit keeping its treading boosters in check while he flailed to see what Maze saw.

"What?" He turned, looking up and down and in every direction he could think of.

"Oh no," Maze said, voice weaker now. Trembling. "Oh, God, no..."

"What?" Cujo repeated. "What's..." He looked up again. The cloud of scarlet swirled just enough to make out a body. Then a face. All the air leaked out of his lungs. He opened his mouth, but words wouldn't come out. He gasped, found some breath, and managed a slight, "Ellen?"

Before he could stop her, Maze shot upward to the floating body.

"Maze," he said, trying to reel in his emotions. "Get away from the blood!"

"No," Maze cried. "It can't be...it can't be...aw goddamn it!"

Maze's mind wasn't on the present danger. Love took over and blinded her to her surroundings. Shock, grief and love. The three things a person must not succumb to during a battle.

Cujo returned his—

He gaped into a cavern of crooked, pointy teeth.

"Shit," he said and told the suit to jet away from the threat. He didn't know if that was a real command or not, but it must have been close enough. The suit shot him to the left before the massive mouth filled with teeth closed over him.

"Maze," Cujo shouted, suit still carrying him away from her and the shark. "Get the hell outta there. It's coming for you!"

Only static greeted him.

"Maze? Respond." He watched the wall of black that had to be the Black Demon shift upward. A long pectoral fin stood out for a moment as a bit of sun from the surface highlighted it. "If you can hear me, jet outta there right now. It's—"

"Pops," Maze said. "She's dead. She's—"

"We'll deal with that later," Cujo said. "Get your ass away from the blood. Now!"

Maze didn't respond and Cujo stopped his suit from sending him farther away. He floated for a few seconds, trying to think of something, anything, he could do while he watched the enormous cryptid shark open its mouth. It didn't move fast, either. Like it was savoring the moment.

"Boss," Benny said. "What's going on?"

"It's here," Cujo managed, watching the giant creature glide toward the surface with its toothy maw wide open.

He couldn't tell if Maze was there or not. The blood was too thick. Even the suit's advanced optics failed to find her.

Regardless, he must try to stop the creature from hurting her.

"Full speed," he told the suit, glaring at the gargantuan black shark. A diabolic silhouette against all that deep blue. "Straight ahead." He lifted his right arm while the suit surged forward like Superman. "Missiles."

The mini missiles emerged from the suit's forearm. He aimed his fist at the moving black wall. "Fire six missiles!"

Immediately a series of silvery bubbles obscured his vision for a second or two. Something he needed to account for in the future, he reckoned.

"DIRECT HIT," the suit announced, startling Cujo a bit.

A few small spirals of scarlet twisted upward from the gargantuan shark. At first, it didn't even appear to be phased by the attack...then the explosions happened.

Cujo's entire view became a giant red cloud.

"Slow," he ordered the suit.

Drifting into the cloud of blood, Cujo positioned himself to be vertical, instead of flying in Superman style. He couldn't see and the suit wasn't telling him anything. It wasn't—

"LARGE LIFEFORM DETECTED. TEN METERS."

"Stop."

The suit glided to a stop in the storm of cryptid blood.

"Maze?"

No answer.

"Fuck," he managed, knowing he was too late. The monster got her. If only he had acted sooner. Maybe—

"I...I don't know where it is, Pops," Maze said and he realized he was hearing fear in her voice for the first time. Real fear. Not just shaken but scared to her core.

Still, he sighed relief. "Stay where you are. I'll find you."

"Sh-she's dead, Pops. All the blood..."

"I know," Cujo said and told his suit to move in slow mode. "Just stand fast, soldier." In a stronger voice he called for Benny, Luna and Wade to return to their original location. "It's here. Not sure where. But it's here."

"Ten-four," Benny said. "On our way."

Blood swirled around Cujo, still too thick to see beyond it, even while moving through the mess. His heart quaked. Every nerve...white hot. It was here. Somewhere. Waiting...

But waiting for what? Yes, it enjoyed toying with its prey. But maybe he really did hurt it with the missiles? Maybe he scared it away and his nerves were just too jacked to realize. His mind playing tricks. Happened all the time, even with highly trained soldiers. The mind was a powerful thing after all.

The cloud of scarlet swirled all around him. Wasn't there supposed to be some sort of current in the ocean? He thought he read or saw something about that not too long ago. Why was the blood just kind of...hanging around?

"Pops? Where are you?"

"On my way. Going through all the blood right now."

"I can see the blood," Maze said. "Huge cloud. You think it's dead?"

"I don't know." The suit didn't detect any lifeforms. So, either the shark was dead, or he hurt it enough to scare it off.

He hoped it was the former rather than the latter. Just let it end now.

"Someone on the boat," Maze said, snapping him out of his thoughts. "Someone killed Ellen."

"I know," Cujo said, trying to keep most of his focus on his surroundings. "We'll get to the bottom of it as soon as—"

"Maze," Benny shouted. "That big fucker is coming for ya! Check your nine!"

"Oh, sh—" Static finished the last word.

"Maze?" Cujo said.

"Fuck," Benny said. "We're comin', Boss. About fifty meters."

"What happened?" Cujo said. "Is she okay? *Maze?*"

"I don't know, Boss. That thing looks like it's just floating there now."

"That's not possible," Reece chimed in. "Sharks need to keep moving or they die."

"Well," Benny said. "This one ain't dyin'."

Cujo blinked. "You said it's above the blood cloud?"

"Yes," Benny said. "But this is really weird, man. Why is it just floating there?"

"Don't know," Cujo said. "My concern is Maze right now."

He ordered the suit to go slowly to the surface. Above, all he saw was swirling cryptid shark blood. Cujo pointed his right arm in a fist upward, mini missiles ready to deploy at a second's notice. His heart bashed itself so hard against his ribs he wondered if he might be having a damn heart attack of all things. Now wouldn't that be hilarious? Big bad cryptid slayer not taken out by a monster, but by an old ticker that survived too many battles unscathed.

He snorted at the thought. It'd be just his luck if—

The blood cleared and he gaped at the side of an enormous shark's head. Its giant mouth opened and closed slightly, appearing to draw in water. Gills, about as long as he was tall, appeared to flap.

"I see you, Boss," Benny said, jolting Cujo out of the terror gripping him, though only for a couple of seconds. "Don't move. I got this big bastard."

But when Cujo opened his mouth to order the suit to stop, all that came out was a thin squeak. And he continued toward the surface.

"Boss," Benny said. "Get out of the way. I got a clear headshot."

Snap out of it, old man, a voice in his head said. A voice he knew well. His grandpa's. "Snap out of it", was one of the man's favorite lines. Even though Cujo knew it was really his own thought, it was Grandpa's voice he heard it in.

Cujo shook his head, and aimed the missiles at the monstrosity's large, black eye. Deep, bleak…emptiness, is what Cujo saw in that eye. A fathomless void where one would go mad looking at it for too long.

"Fire six," Cujo said, suit still propelling him toward the surface.

All six shot from the ring around the suit's forearm and, in rill of bubbles, zipped at the Black Demon.

He smiled, knowing an eye injury could be fatal. If nothing else, it'd be wounded enough to dispatch easier.

But he didn't take into account he was still moving upward. The physics of the attack never entered his mind, until four or five of the missiles cut grooves over the shark's head and one missed completely.

"Fuck," he managed.

"Boss, *dude*, what the—shit, look out!"

It was like the beast had been sleeping the entire time. The giant shark's head swished from side to side. Before Cujo could really get his bearings, it jetted away from him and dove until it disappeared in the deep, dark waters.

"Get to the boat," Cujo said.

"It's at one thousand feet," Reece said.

"Where the hell were you like five minutes ago?" Cujo said, unable to keep the anger from his voice.

"Comms went down. Sorry. Some kind of interference."

"Were you banging Ross again?" Benny said. "You little minx, you."

"Shut up, Benny," Cujo said. "Do you have a link on Maze?"

"The Black Demon stopped at almost the two thousand feet mark."

"Reece," Cujo said. "Can you see where Maze is? You have links on all our suits, right?"

"Yes. Sorry. Trying to keep track of everything. I'm only one person."

"Where the hell is Ross?"

"Checking why the comms were interrupted."

Cujo frowned. "Does he think it's foul play?"

"He's not sure. Found her."

His heart kicked up a beat or two. "Where?" Cujo glanced around but didn't see anything except ocean and the other three of his team.

"She's on the boat."

"*What?*"

"That's where I'm tracking her suit," Reece said.

"Boss," Benny said. "You want me to go check on her?"

"No." He sighed. "Listen, all of you. Ellen is dead. I don't know how, but there was a lot of blood."

"Oh, no. One of the people from the other boat, you think?" Luna asked.

"I don't know," Cujo said. "Not going to speculate until—"

"The Black Demon is moving fast back toward you all," Reece interrupted. "Too fast. I'm lagging five seconds trying to track it. Ten seconds."

"Ah, shit, man," Benny said. "What the fuck, now? We got some crazy shit happening on our boat and now this thing is doing…what, exactly?"

"Breaching," Wade said, almost a whisper.

"What?" Cujo said.

Wade cleared his throat. "I've watched Shark Week for years. Great whites will shoot out of the water to catch seals. It's called breaching, I think."

"What does that have to do with—" but Reece cut Benny off.

"You better figure something out because you have less than two minutes before it eats all of you."

"Spread out," Cujo shouted. "As far as you can. Give it space. If it's trying to do that breach thing, it'll shoot right by us. Target the tail. Lasers, missiles, whatever. Annihilate the tail."

Everyone jetted away from the spot they were floating in and formed a rough circle with an eighty-foot radius. Cujo wasn't sure if the formation was wide enough, but it would have to do.

"Should be directly under you now," Reece said.

Cujo glanced down but didn't see anything, nor did his suit detect any large lifeforms. Silence stretched out for a handful of seconds.

"It stopped," Reece said. "I don't…" A pause. "Wait it's moving north. Your right, Cujo. About one hundred feet below."

"Oh, this is just lovely," Benny spouted. "It already knew we were planning an ambush."

"It's smarter than we think it is," Luna said. Her voice was barely above a whisper.

"Reece," Cujo said. "Location."

"Still moving north. Still at around one hundred feet."

"LIFEFORMS DETECTED," their suits chimed in unison.

"Oh, what the fuck now?" Benny said.

Cujo looked up, blinked and said, "Ellen…"

About six or seven sharks of various sizes, attracted by Ellen's blood, were tearing her body apart. Blood spread in a large cloud.

Cujo closed his eyes and lowered his head. Tears burned behind his eyelids.

"Oh," Luna said. "Oh, no."

"Goddamn it," Benny said.

"No," Wade said.

Cujo, unable to wipe his tears away because of the suit, endured the trickling streaks tickling his face for a few seconds.

"Maze is on the boat alone," Luna said. "What if—"

LARGE LIFEFORM DETECTED.

Cujo blinked, glanced around. "Reece?"

"Our links are sputtering. Hold on."

"What the fuck does that mean?" Benny said. "Sputtering? What the hell?"

"Shut it," Cujo said and squinted at the vast darkness below them. "Someone is messing with our comms. Our links." He looked at his team. "I think someone planned for this to happen."

"What?" Luna said. "Why?"

"See," Benny said. "It's Mary's dad, dude! He sent us all out here to die and she killed Ellen."

Cujo clenched his jaw, not wanting to believe what Benny said, but at the same time, it made sense. Well, kind of. There was still the motive part. Why would Mary's father send them out to save people, knowing the Black Demon was around, and let his own daughter go? That part didn't sit well with him.

And now Ellen was dead. Throat slashed and ripped apart by sharks.

Whoever was involved would get what's coming to them tenfold. If they made it out of the ocean alive, anyway. He also had his suspicions. Brax was number one. Who else would be able to block comms to the suits?

"It's directly under you," Reece said, voice cracking a bit.

"Shit," Cujo said.

"I can't tell if it's in breach position or just floating there."

"Why is it doing this?" Wade said. "We're sitting ducks. You'd think it would try to eat us by now."

Cujo, staring into the dark blue abyss below said, "I don't know."

"The Black Demon," Reece said. "It's not exactly known for its predictability. It knows you're there. It's watching you. Maybe it's trying to figure out what you are. I don't know. What I do know is it has a tendency to play with people's minds. You need to outthink it. Be two steps ahead."

Silence drifted among the remaining team.

Cujo frowned into the dark fathoms. "We hit it with all we got."

A blip of further silence and Benny swam over to him. "What are you saying?"

Cujo waved his right arm, so he faced Benny fully. "Instead of trying to trick it into an ambush or play stupid games, we attack full force. What we should've done in the first place." He glanced at the others. "Your target is its tail."

"Boss, I don't think—"

"That's actually a good plan," Reece chimed in.

"I—" Benny began and paused. "Wait, what?"

"It's a good plan. The Black Demon is toying with you all, for whatever reason. It's playing a game and expects you to keep trying to outrun or ambush it. It knows it's bigger than you and can kill you at any time. It appears to thrive on the games. Like leaving those people in the other charter to eventually drown. Maybe it was waiting for the boat to actually begin to sink before breaking it apart and eating them. I don't know. Like I said before, this is one cryptid I know little about." She paused for a couple of seconds. "Attacking it might just jar it enough for you to get the upper hand."

"And if it isn't jarred?" Wade said.

"Then you are all shark food," Reece said.

"Damn," Benny said. "Reece ain't playing anymore."

Reece, obviously ignoring Benny, said, "Hit it fast and hard and don't let up. Confuse it. Shock it. I bet there is nothing in the ocean that has ever tried to attack it. It's the top of the food chain and arrogant."

Cujo nodded. "Thanks, Reece." He gave his remaining team a once over. "Here's the plan. The three of you hit that big bastard head on with missiles. I'll come in on its flank and laser cut its tail off."

"Hold on," Luna said. "If this thing can breathe, or whatever, without moving, cutting its tail off will still leave it alive. Right?"

"Correct," Reece said. "But you will also be able to disable it and kill it." She cleared her throat. "Oh! Get a blood sample, if you can. I don't know if there are more than one of these types of shark, but I would like to know for sure. Might help in future operations."

"Oh, for fuck sake," Benny said. "You and your blood samples."

"How are we supposed to extract the samples?" Cujo asked. "The suits aren't equipped with needles or anything."

But Reece didn't respond.

After a few seconds, Cujo frowned. "Reece?"

Again, no response.

"Comms must be down again," Luna said.

"So," Wade said. "What do we do? How are going to collect a blood sample?"

"We're not," Cujo said. "We follow the plan. You three attack head on and I'll cut its tail off. You are the distraction."

"Oh," Benny said. "Thanks a lot, asshole..."

TWENTY-ONE

At the same time Luna, Wade and Benny jetted down toward the mountain of shark waiting for them, Cujo shot away to the south about fifty meters.

This was it. All or nothing.

And, if he was wrong, they would all die. The Black Demon, such a crafty creature, could no doubt gobble everyone up without a second thought. Reece might be on to something with it being arrogant and used to always winning. Its guard was down. It thought it always had the upper hand. No matter what species. Even orcas, which were supposed be the most tactful marine life ever to exist. If that was true or not, he didn't know. It felt right, though.

He looped back around.

"What depth is the bastard, Reece?"

"One-thousand-two-hundred feet."

"Thanks. You tracking my location?"

"Yes," Reece said.

"Good. Let me know when I'm within fifty feet."

"Will do. Be careful."

Cujo smirked and thought, *Nothing ever gets done when people are careful.*

"You are currently at the same depth as the Black Demon," Reece said. "Three hundred feet away."

He slipped through the dark water like a torpedo and, for the first time since entering the ocean, he wasn't afraid. Maybe he was getting used to the bleak vastness of it. Or, rather, he found himself in a place he often did in battle. Ultra-focused on the goal. The heart of the mission. So focused that nothing else mattered much. All that mattered was the target and eliminating it in the most efficient way possible.

"One hundred feet and closing," Reece said, though her voice was like background noise. He heard it. He understood it. But it wasn't the main focus. The target. That was the main focus. With everything going on, he lost his focus.

"Eighty feet," Reece said.

"Holy shit," Benny shouted, quaking the inside of Cujo's helmet.

"Look out," Luna said. "It's—"

Static drowned out the rest.

"Benny? Luna?" Cujo glanced around, still heading full speed toward the target.

Fear wormed its way in again. His heart thudded. Heavy. A constant bludgeon to his ribs. Like being punched repeatedly from the inside.

"Where are you guys?" Wade said. "M-My suit is malfunctioning, I think. Can't see anything!"

"Just stay where you are, Wade," Cujo said. "I'm on my way."

"You are two hundred feet below your target," Reece said. "It's on the move all of a sudden."

"What about Benny and Luna?"

A slight pause…

"Fine, Boss," Benny said.

"Almost got eaten," Luna said, "but okay."

"It was like a goddamn statue until we got closer," Benny said. "Then it just went nuts." A pause. "Snagged Wade, too. Little fella got all mixed up."

"Shut up," Wade said.

"Where is it?" Luna said. "It's like it disappeared."

"I'm detecting a large lifeform in your vicinity, Cujo." Reece said.

"Where?" Cujo said, trying to look everywhere at once, surprised his suit didn't blare it before Reece did.

"I…I'm not sure. It's either moving too fast for the satellite to read or—supernatural—it—out!"

Cujo frowned. "Didn't copy, Reece. Repeat."

A few blips of Reece's voice were soon drowned in static. Then absolute silence.

"What the fuck?" Benny said.

"Must be another comms issue," Luna said.

"Yeah," Cujo said. "Stay alert. I—"

"LARGE LIFEFORM DETECTED," his suit chimed. "TWENTY-FIVE FEET BELOW."

Cujo blinked. "Shit." He shifted directions, cutting to the east.

"…west…dive!" Reece stuttered though the static.

"Boss?" Benny said. "What's going on?"

Cujo didn't answer and instead implemented the words that managed to make it through all the buzzing and crackling. He instructed the suit to deep dive and veered to the west. All in rapid thrust.

"Diving," Cujo said. "Moving west."

A breath of silence. "I took the words to mean it's on your western flank and to dive straight down," Luna said.

Cujo sucked in a sharp breath as if slapped. If Luna was right, then he was jetting through the water over one hundred miles per hour directly at the Black Demon.

"LARGE LIFEFORM DETECTED," the suit blared. "FORTY METERS AND CLOSING."

"Cuj—surf—!" Reece's voice sputtered through the static.

"Wait," Benny said. "Does she want you to go surfing?"

Cujo rolled his eyes and commanded his suit to haul ass to the surface. It swerved in a long upward arc and, within a few seconds he screamed as a cavern of teeth flashed in front of him briefly.

"What?" Benny said. "What's going on?"

As soon as his heart settled, Cujo said, "Oh, you know, I was almost fish food. But other than that…"

"Oh, look, he thinks he's a comedian, guys," Benny said. "Dramatic eyeroll. Weak sauce, Boss."

"Stay focused," Cujo said. "It's heading your way, I think."

"Goddamn it," Benny said.

Cujo slowed his progress to the surface until he was about thirty feet below. He looked down in the darkness. There was only death down there. Fathoms of horrors. And was it watching him right now? Instead of going after the rest of the team, could it be hiding in the darkness just waiting? Waiting for what, well, who knew for sure. It apparently loved to play games.

A small school of shiny fish darted by, but other than that, the ocean might as well be lifeless.

"Benny, Luna, and Wade," he said. "You all still okay?" It wasn't just that, either. He suddenly felt too alone. A tiny speck in a vast, dark world.

"Yeah, Boss," Benny said.

"All good," Wade said. "What do you want us to do?"

"I second Wade," Luna said. "We need a different plan."

"With comms down again," Cujo said, "we don't know where it is."

"So, should we go back to the boat, then?" Benny said. "Figure out what's up with Maze and why Ellen is dead? Maybe get our good weapons like we should've done before jumping into this nasty ass puddle?"

"It'll destroy the boat," Cujo said. "And eat everyone on it. We won't be in our suits and will be less protected."

"I hate it when you're right," Benny grumbled.

Cujo stared into the dark fathoms of the Pacific Ocean. A frown creased his face.

"It likes to play games. Toy with its prey." His frown deepened into a glare. "I say let's turn the tables."

"What are you talking about, Boss?"

Still glaring into the darkness, Cujo smirked. "We play a game."

TWENTY-TWO

"Wade, Benny," Cujo said, making his way toward their location. "I want you both to dive to eight hundred feet. Luna, I need you to stay with me near the surface."

"What the hell would that achieve?" Benny said. "Why split us up again? I think if we had all gone in guns blazing instead of you breaking off from the team to cut the tail, we might've kicked its ass."

"Maybe," Cujo said. "It's smarter than I gave it credit for. But I want you all to pay close attention. This is what we're going to do."

LIFEFORMS DETECTED, the suit informed him. FIFTY-EIGHT FEET NORTHEAST. DEPTH: TEN METERS.

"Might be coming up to you all soon," Cujo said.

He glanced around, making sure the suit wasn't having some sort of a glitch and the Black Demon was stalking him.

"Are you detecting an approaching lifeform?"

"Yes," Luna said.

He slowed his speed until he was about fifteen feet away and drifted to them.

"Well," Benny said. "It's about damn time."

"Shush," Cujo said. "Okay, the object of this game is to confuse the hell out of it by splitting up in pairs. First, it won't know which to go after. Wade and Benny, I changed my mind. Instead of eight hundred feet, go a little below five. I want you to move in S patterns, changing it up every twenty seconds by moderately ascending toward the surface. Go one hundred feet."

"So, if we're at five hundred, go to four hundred?" Wade asked.

"Yep. Then, as soon as you reach that depth, dive fast back to five hundred. Every minute I want you to full stop."

A lengthy silence followed and Cujo wondered if he sounded a bit crazy to them. Like he'd lost whatever marbles he might have still had clacking around in his head. The thought gave him pause. He never really second guessed himself or his own cognizance before. Maybe a couple of times, but never full stop like now.

You're over sixty, Hoss, he heard his grandpa say. *Things'll start gettin' a bit fuzzy up in the ol' attic.*

Cujo blinked and said, "You two do that while Luna and I will make as much noise and movement near the surface."

"And...how's this supposed to stop the giant shark cryptid monster?" Benny said. "Speaking of monster, has anyone been keeping an eye out for the big bastard?"

"I already told you. Confuse the hell out of it. It'll do something uncharacteristic. Make a mistake."

"Sounds like wishful thinking," Luna said.

"It is," Cujo said and sighed. "I'm guessing here, but I feel like it's right and the only thing, we can do. A gut feeling."

"If there was ever a time I wished Reece was jabbering in my ear," Benny said, "it's now." He chuckled humorlessly. "Boss, this plan doesn't make sense."

"I know," Cujo said. "Just do it. When we see it begin acting erratically, that's when we attack. We want it disoriented and—"

LARGE LIFEFORM APPROACHING. TWO HUNDRED FEET BELOW.

"Ah, shit," Benny said. "So much for your crazy plan, Boss."

"Stick with the plan," Cujo said. "Game time."

"Shit," someone said under their breath. He wasn't sure who.

"Luna," Cujo said, head to the surface now. "Wade and Benny, you thrust fifty feet away from this spot and dive to five hundred."

"Got it," Benny said. "Let's go, lil'fella!"

Wade sighed. "Shut up."

They jetted away, leaving only Luna and Cujo.

"Rapid boost west at an eighty-degree angle."

LARGE LIFEFORM DETECTED. SIXTY FEET BELOW.

"Make sense?" Cujo added.

"Yes."

"Go!"

They commanded their suits to do just as Cujo ordered and shot through the water so fast it took Cujo a second or two to realize they were gone.

"Go for thirty feet below the surface," he told Luna.

"On it." She surged upward.

Cujo glanced down but there sprawled only darkness. Not an empty darkness, though. Oh, no. Not that. Not here.

He was about to order his suit to rapid boost to thirty feet to the surface when something glittered in the vast dark below. He frowned.

"Cujo," Luna said. "You okay?"

"Y-Yeah," he said. "Just...there's something—"

And then it emerged from the black depths. Slow, purposeful.

A massive mouth lined with rows, at least six deep, of long, glimmering teeth. He had time enough to notice not all the teeth were

101

shaped the same. Some resembled a great white, thick and triangular, while others appeared to be more like jagged needles.

"I didn't copy all of that," Luna said, breaking him from his reverie. "Are you—"

"Move eighty feet to the north," Cujo said, staring at the cavern of teeth making its way closer and closer. "I don't know what the hell it's doing. Just be careful. It might—"

There was no time.

The moment those final words were out of his mouth, the cavern of teeth became his home. A split second.

The suit beeped. Red words scrolled across the visor of his helmet. PRESSURE WARNING! PUNCTURE WARNING!

"Shit," Cujo said, realizing he was in the mouth of the Black Demon.

Terror snagged his heart like an old, rusty hook and tugged hard. Submerged in absolute darkness, Cujo struggled to find his bearings.

DO YOU WISH TO ACTIVATE NIGHT VISION? the suit asked.

"Yes," he said. "For fuck sake, yes!"

The visor flickered, but where he was expecting a green hue to see in the dark, everything was clear. Well, maybe twilight clear, anyway. A bit shadowed and tinged with a gray. He floated from side to side, up and down, thumping into the insides of the Black Demon's mouth. He gaped down the monster's throat, watched the gills work, and shivered.

Holy shit, I'm inside its mouth, he thought.

"I'm inside its mouth," he repeated out loud.

"Cu-o?" someone said. He couldn't tell who through all the static. "Where—you? I—at—copy?"

"I'm inside the Black Demon's mouth," he said. "I repeat, the big bastard ate me."

"The fuck?" Benny sprang through the helmet's speakers.

"CF6," he said. "My team. Listen…" He sighed and glanced around, not sure what to say.

"CF6?" Benny said. "I dig it! Deep in my soul…"

Cujo sighed a second time. Leave it to Benny to make it weird.

"Shut up," he said to Benny. To everyone, he sighed, and continued what he meant to say. "Listen, I want you all to retreat. We need better weapons than the suits provide and those are on the boat." He cleared his throat; tears welled in his eyes. "Retreat. Find out what happened to Ellen and Maze. And, if you can, gear up and take this big son of a bitch out."

Silence strung out for at least a minute.

"What if we can't find you?" Luna said.

Cujo smiled. Tears squiggled down his cheeks. "Then leave me be and move on to another mission. It has been my pleasure to command each and every one of you."

"Oo-Rah," Wade said.

"Hoo-ah," Benny said.

"Hoo-ah," Luna said.

Cujo closed his eyes…

TWENTY-THREE

He didn't know much about sharks other than what he saw in movies or documentaries, which was slim at best because learning about sharks wasn't something high on his priority list.

So, why didn't the Black Demon swallow him? Could sharks swallow? Or did bits and pieces of their prey just kind of drift down the gullet? While he drifted, floated and bumped along within the monster's mouth, it was the only thought which wriggled through his terror. He was inside a giant shark's mouth, after all. Every now and then, his suit would scrape against one of the smaller back row teeth. Slight vibration and a subtle *reeee*'s made it through the protective layers of the suit.

Alone…

His gaze drifted to the gills. They flapped without pause. Sometimes fast, though slow for the most part.

"We're almost to the boat, Boss," Benny said.

"Could be an ambush waiting," Wade said.

Cujo blinked, drawing his attention away from the gills. "Each of you pick a different entry point. If there is an ambush, they would most likely be the main point of entry we used to leave the boat."

"There are different entry points?" Benny asked.

"I think so," Cujo said. "If not, you have to figure out another way. But I was sure Reece said something about more than one entry point for a boat that size."

A long pause followed and Cujo found himself staring at the gills again.

"You think it might be those people we rescued?" Luna said.

Still staring at the gills, Cujo sighed. "I don't know."

"How you holdin' up, Boss?"

He smiled a bit. "Oh, feeling a bit chummy, I guess."

Someone snorted, probably Benny. "That's like the worst dad joke ever." A few chuckles flowed out of the suit's speakers.

"We're about twenty feet below the boat and closing," Luna said. There was no emotion in her voice. No fear. Nothing but extreme focus. He caught all this in her flat, no-nonsense tone.

"I'm going to check the boat and see how many entry points there are," Benny said.

"Wade and I are holding position," Luna said. "Awaiting command."

Cujo, thumping, drifting, scraping inside the Black Demon's maw, nodded. "Infiltrate and illuminate all hostiles. I repeat…*all* hostiles."

A pause.

Finally, Wade, the only one who responded, said, "Roger that."

"In the meantime," Cujo said, "I'll try to figure a way out of this thing."

"Why not just use your laser and cut through it?" Benny said. "Dude, you could kill it right fuckin' now."

Cujo nodded. Good point, but, at the same time, he saw what little good the missiles did. Were they also fools to believe the suit's laser would cut through the creature's skin? Everyone kept forgetting the Black Demon wasn't like any other shark. There was something seriously off about it. Something almost supernatural...

"I'll figure something out," Cujo repeated. "Finish the mission. I'll meet up with you all shortly."

No one responded, not even Wade with a "Roger that".

Cujo sighed and stared once again at the gills.

Benny, of course, was right. He was in the beast's mouth. Probably one of the most vulnerable spots of the thing, for all he knew. Maybe inside would be different than outside, right? Softer whereas the monster's skin was like its armor. No wonder it lived for so long. Nothing could penetrate its skin or whatever protected the ancient cryptid.

But from inside...

It had briefly crossed his mind before, sure, but now...now...

"Boarding," Luna said.

"Rear," Benny said. "Boarding."

"Still searching for a port of entry," Wade said.

"If you can't find one," Benny said, "try the stern if there is one. They won't be expecting that."

"Roger that," Wade said.

"Be careful," Cujo said, voice barely above a whisper. All he could do was hope things went okay topside. They were his team, after all. His family.

Cujo stared at the gills. The longer he did, the more rage spilled through him. He clenched his jaw; gritted his teeth. No, he refused to go out like this. It was playing with him. Had to be. Why else hadn't he been swallowed down? Certainly, there was a way for sharks to swallow without tongues, right? He didn't know.

He glared at the gills. He watched them flap at different speeds. Watched them pause, then ripple. Watched them move as though they had minds of their own. He clunked against sharp teeth and thumped along the pink padding of the monster's mouth.

"Not today, motherfucker," he said in something close to a growl and thrust his left arm at the gills. "Fire," he said.

The laser shot out of his forearm and sliced through the gills like they were nothing. A flash of blue and red and suddenly he found himself in a cloud of scarlet.

Instantly, the environment changed inside the shark's mouth. The gradual back and forth motion became chaotic thrashing. Cujo was flung in every direction, bouncing off of everything so hard the suit shrilled alarm after alarm. Still, he kept his focus on the shredded gills, which flapped around like silk sheets in a tornado. Wild and flailing, giving him more reason to believe they might, indeed, have minds of their own. As though they were the only things in pain, rather than the cryptid shark as a whole.

Still, he cursed himself for not just blasting the laser through the roof of its mouth into his brain. Killing it. With all the thrashing, he couldn't get himself positioned long enough for a good shot.

It could have been all over right then, he thought.

Lapse in judgment. He hated when that happened. People died for such lapses. Thankfully it was extremely rare throughout his career.

Oh well. Only one thing left to do now…

He rapid boosted through the flailing gills into the open waters of the Pacific Ocean.

About one hundred feet, he slowed and risked a glance back.

The Black Demon still thrashed. Its long tail whipped and sliced through the water. Heavy pressure, underwater waves, whatever it was called, pummeled him which triggered the suit's pressure alarm.

His mind screamed at him to get the hell out of there. Get to the boat and figure out what was going on with comms. He could try and cut its tail off right now, but with it whipping like that, he wasn't sure if he'd manage the task or merely piss the bastard off more.

No.

Instead, he turned and rapid boosted out of the area.

"Show me home," he told the suit. In training, Brax often referred to the point of origin as "home". The suit wasn't very good at GPS stuff, but it could find where its dock location was well enough.

Well, Cujo hoped anyway.

He also hoped, without any blood, he would lose the Black Demon for a bit. Or, hell, maybe it would drown now that its gills were shredded? This he hoped for most of all. If—

Something massive and blacker than the darkest night slipped across in front of him.

"Stop," he said, heart stuttering, and immediately wished he hadn't.

The suit came to a full stop, smooshing his face against the helmet's visor so hard he about broke his nose. If his head was tilted just right...

Instead, it felt like someone was punching his right eye in slow motion. Hurt like hell. He growled, trying to ignore the pain while the stupid suit finally came to a stop. It took about three seconds to fully stop but felt like an eternity.

The pressure on his face decreased and he peeled himself away. The visor, sheened with his sweat and skin oils, blinked.

LARGE LIFEFORM DETECTED. FORTY METERS SOUTHWEST.

Cujo sucked in a sharp breath and glanced around but the ocean was the same vast dark blue emptiness as before. With all the commotion, whatever sea life in the area probably got the hell out of the way. Especially with such a huge predator haunting the waters. Everything living knew to steer clear of the monster.

A thing that should not be.

But was and lurking somewhere nearby.

Forty meters? How many feet was that? Like one hundred feet? Something like that. His brain was too frazzled to really care. He needed to figure out a plan, because, obviously, the Black Demon wasn't about to let him go so easily.

He imagined, though briefly, he'd get eaten again so he could do what he should have done the first time.

Cut the bastard to pieces from the inside out.

Even a battle-hardened mind skipped a beat from time to time. No matter how much logic screamed at a person, sometimes decisions were made out of immediate necessity. Stress always played a part too. An opportunity missed.

But, if the monstrous shark was half as smart as he thought it was, it wouldn't swallow him. Rather, it'd chomp him in half and leave his remains twitching in its wake for other sharks to shred to pieces. Then it would go after the boat.

LARGE LIFEFORM DETECTED. WEST. SIXTY FEET AND CL— TEN FEET AND—

Cujo blinked, followed the compass from his visor and came face to massive grin with the Black Demon.

"Shit," he managed before all the air whooshed out of him.

It didn't move for the longest time. Though, just as Cujo found a way to breathe again, it shifted a bit backward and to the side. A single, black eye. A darkest fathom glared back at him. Onyx oblivion. Cujo looked away every couple of seconds because staring into such bleak darkness for too long could surely turn a person insane.

What was its game now? No doubt it was pissed. Maybe it was having trouble living with its severed gi—

Cujo's eyes widened when he noticed what the Black Demon really wanted him to see.

The severed gills…they…they were whole again. He watched them flap in unison and returned his attention to that eye the size of a large truck tire.

"You can heal yourself," he said, gaping at the creature. "That's how you've lived for so long. You can heal yourself."

Not only that…it could do so in record time.

The Black Demon slipped across his view. A long wall of black until the blue of the ocean struck him with all its brilliance. He didn't know where it went or what he should do. If it could heal itself, well…that was game over. Right? How could they kill a thing that's centuries old, intelligent, and healed itself on a whim? How?

And why didn't it kill him right then?

Why just…

Cujo sucked in a sharp breath.

The boat.

He checked his location in proximity to the large charter boat. "Fuck."

The boat was a little over one hundred meters northeast. Three hundred feet or so, if he had his math about right. Although he could be wrong. What if it was farther than three hundred feet? What if the tracking system was damaged or tossed overboard? What if the suit was wrong and he shot right by the boat without realizing it?

There was no other choice now. He would have to trust the technology to lead him back to the boat before the shark found it first.

The Black Demon had tricked him. Still playing its game. It was using him up. Weakening him mentally, emotionally and physically. It wanted him to suffer. Demon. No other word was more apt.

He ordered his suit into hyper boost mode. The one speed Brax warned about during training. Cujo couldn't remember exactly how fast hyper boost got, but he remembered Brax telling him to use it only in emergencies. The suit hissed around him. Something vibrated along his spine. Soft whirring.

Just as his brain latched onto the fact he was moving at relatively warp speed, a whale drifted in front of him. Cujo gasped and tried to aim his body downward to dive under it, but he was moving too fast and no matter what he tried he remained in a straight line directly at the whale. A humpback, maybe.

"*Movemovemove,*" Cujo said in a single breath.

When it was apparent the large whale wasn't going to move, Cujo clenched his jaw and braced for—

He didn't even have time to close his eyes when he plunged into the side of the whale like a torpedo. A melee of blubber, blood, organs, and bone. He was barely able to register all this before he shot out of the opposite side in a kaleidoscope of gore.

He couldn't look back to see the carnage. Movement wasn't an option. He focused his attention ahead. If he was going fast enough to shoot through a thick whale like it's nothing, it meant an island or rocks could sprout up and he'd be dead. The impact would be the end, even with the suit. Maybe that was what Brax meant by using hyper boost. Why it was so damn dangerous. You couldn't control anything while in hyper boost.

He was about one hundred feet from the boat. At least he hoped so.

Sixty feet to the location of the boat, Cujo slowed the suit to high boost, then medium. Though going from hyper to medium speed felt like he was travelling in slow motion now.

Not fast enough, he thought. *If it—*

There was no time to react.

It came out of nowhere.

TWENTY-FOUR

"PRESSURE WARNING."

Cujo, caught in a flurry of bubbles, couldn't tell what was going on other than something had him in its jaws.

Something big.

"C-jo," Reece's voice stuttered through the speakers. "Hold on. We—out what—not it. The boat!"

"What the fuck are you talking about?" he said, though didn't get a reply.

The pressure warning didn't sound again. Only the faint, rushing howl of water filtering through the water intakes.

Cujo pushed away from the jaws holding him by the upper torso and chest, just enough to turn his head.

"Holy shit," he said, heart slamming in his throat.

He caught a bunch of black, yes, but there was also a splash of white. It wasn't the Black Demon trying to eat him, but a killer whale. An orca. Big one too. Though nowhere near the size of the massive cryptid shark. Big enough to puncture a hole in the suit, though. That much he was sure of.

Using the suit's strength to his advantage, Cujo began to pry himself out of the orca's mouth.

All in vain.

Before he could apply any force, the jaws opened, and he shot forward. The suit stabilized just in time for him to catch a glimpse of the orca as it dove below him.

"LIFEFORM DETECTED. THIRTY FEET BELOW."

Cujo opened his mouth to tell the suit to hyper boost the hell away from the area when another orca blasted out of the dark blue and slammed into him hard enough to send him flipping and flailing through the water like a ragdoll being shot out of a cannon. Once the suit managed to stabilize, he didn't even have time to breathe before a blur of white and black side swiped him. He spun like being on one of those old merry-go-rounds. The suit beeped.

'Minor shoulder damage' scrolled across the visor in yellow warning letters.

"Fuck," he said, waiting for the suit to stabilize again and trying not to blow chunks everywhere.

Pain throbbed all over his body from all the bumps and bruises.

A pod of orcas found him and, like a seal, they were playing with him a bit. Confusing him. Weakening him. Just like…

…like the Black Demon.

"Reece, you there?"

Static followed, then only the steady beeping of the suit and his own breathing. Until now, he was able to ignore it. The breathing. But now…now…

It was damn near maddening.

"Benny?"

No reply.

"Maze?"

No reply.

"Luna?"

No reply.

"Wade?"

No reply.

He listened to his own breathing and glanced around for the pod of orcas. His heart thrummed. His stomach lurched like a greasy, green glob.

Once more, loneliness spread throughout him like the cancer it was. Nothing but darkness below and endless blue surrounding him.

Go, his grandfather's voice boomed in his head. *Idiot boy! Move your ass!*

Cujo blinked, and spared another glance around. Where were they? The orcas. Why…

It didn't appear all at once, but rather gradually through the deep blue. An obsidian god approaching the interloper. Slowly, it drifted closer. Every now and then a bit of light would catch the gleam of one black eye or the other giving the monster an even more sinister appearance. Lamplights submerged in oblivion.

The demon didn't go to the boat. It tricked him again. Still playing its game. Like the orcas, it was trying to disorientate him. Confuse him. Weaken his body and mind.

"LARGE LIFEFORM DETECTED. EIGHTY FEET."

Cujo glared at the monster slipping ever closer. "Okay, motherfucker." He lifted both arms, fists aimed at the Black Demon. "Let's do this."

It slowed to a stop at about fifty feet away. Its head swayed slowly back and forth. Its mouth opened and closed, revealing the first and longest row of teeth. Maybe it was weighing its chances. Maybe it had another trick up its gills.

Didn't matter.

He ordered both the laser and remaining six mini-missiles to fire. The missiles struck the creature first. Its head whipped back and forth, up and down, mouth snapping, teeth exploding from one of the missiles.

Cujo roared and sliced the laser across the Black Demon's gaping mouth. The laser separated the lower jaw from the upper by a few sinews of flesh. The lower jaw dangled and flapped while the monster thrashed and shot forward. Cujo boosted to the side a second before the shark crashed into him.

Heart bashing itself into his ribs, he spun and slashed the laser across one of those fathomless, onyx eyes.

The massive shark thrashed in a storm of bubbles and blood. Its long tail whipped, sending a surge of water which shoved Cujo farther and farther away. Then, all at once, it stopped moving and sank head-first into the deep.

Cujo frowned and watched until the cryptid shark disappeared into the deep.

He waited a moment, pretty sure the thing was playing him again. Did sharks sink when they died or float belly-up like other fish? He wasn't totally sure, but he thought they sank.

Ten minutes slipped by and, gradually, relief trickled in. He did it. The big bastard was dead.

Cujo gave the Black Demon's watery grave a final glance, turned and made his way to the charter boat and his team.

That was, if he still had a team now…

TWENTY-FIVE

He tried calling to them again when he reached the charter.

Nothing.

Darkness gripped his heart like cold, skeletal claws for fear they'd ended up like Ellen: throat slashed and dumped into the ocean to feed the sharks.

Cujo shook his head, trying to clear the thought. Couldn't let his emotions get the better of him. Especially now.

"Reece," he said while drifting closer to the boat's bow. "If you can hear me, this might be my last transmission. I don't know what to expect on the boat, but I'm about to find out. If something happens to me, I want to let you know you were a treat to work with and your father would be proud of you." He sighed. "Just as I'm proud of you. I leave you in charge of building a new team. Over…and out."

Again, only static greeted him.

A large shark, though smaller than a great white, glided by.

Cujo drew in a breath and blew it out slowly. He was now the right side of the bow. Even from a few feet underwater he could see no way of getting aboard this way. He patrolled the entire perimeter of the boat and found only two ways on. The back, near the propellers, where a ladder was mounted, and another ladder off on the left side. Nearly six feet from each other from what he could tell.

A bottle neck, in other words. So, if there was an ambush waiting for the team, it would be easy pickings once they exited their suits.

The people they'd rescued from the bobbing charter.

Someone mentioned them earlier. Benny? Maze? He couldn't remember. He thought about those people now. Whoever mentioned them before was right. They weren't who Cujo thought they were. Hell, who Reece and the team thought they were either.

And who sent the team to rescue those people…?

Mary's father.

But why? What was the man's stake in killing off the Cryptid Force Six? Did someone pay him? If so, who? And who did they piss off enough to get them killed?

With the Black Demon dead, he let the questions circle in his mind while he surfaced and reached for the ladder at the back of the boat.

He steeled himself for what he might encounter on deck and climbed onto the boat.

In the water, the suits moved without strain by the wearer. Outside of the water, though, was a whole other story. It took a bit of effort to walk to the dock for his Devil 1 suit. The other suits stood in their own docks. Before he moved to step out of his suit, he noticed a small spray of blood on the floor in front of one of the docks.

Cujo blinked.

"They were ambushed right here," he whispered. "As soon as their suits opened."

He stepped backward and glanced around. The deck appeared empty. But he was in the covered area where the suits and equipment were stored. Wouldn't take much for someone to hide effectively.

"Shit," he said.

His gaze drifted to the duffle bags holding the team's preferred weapons. If he could somehow slip out of the suit and get to one of those bags, he might have a chance.

Unless the bastards killed everyone and fled. Maybe they figured the Black Demon had killed Cujo since he—

"LIFEFORMS DETECTED. SURROUNDING. PROXIMITY THIRTEEN FEET AND CLOSING."

Cujo's heart skipped a beat. Nope. Never mind. The intruders were still on the boat.

His gaze snapped back to the duffle bags. There were doors on the left and right. Both shut. Also, a door in the far back leading down to the living quarters. The only real opening was the overhead he'd entered through.

"SIX FEET AND CLOSING," the suit announced.

Cujo clenched his jaw, turned and pulled the suit's dock away from the wall. He shoved it toward the opening, though it didn't block as much as he hoped. Using the strength of the suit, and moving way slower than he wanted, he pushed a dock containing a suit in front of the door on the right.

Sweat sheened his face and trickled down the small of his back. Every step, every movement using the suit was a chore. It wasn't built to walk or be land worthy at all, even if it was supposed to mimic your movements. Brax failed in this department. Maybe the other Devil suits were more amphibious?

Cujo managed to slide another dock in front of the door on the left just as the latch began to move.

He turned, saw two silhouettes approaching the overhead opening, and shoved a final dock in that direction. The silhouettes jumped back. One appeared to draw a gun.

Cujo lurched to the nearest duffle bag and ordered the suit to open. It hissed and split open.

He sprang out, tripped over something, and fell hard on the bags.

There were so many sounds now. The salt in the air struck him like a heavy fist over and over. So much noise compared to being in the suit. Hard to think. The heat. Everything. Too much. All of it pummeling him in heavy succession.

He roared, fighting the disorientation and unzipped the nearest duffle bag.

Crashing drew his attention to the door at his right. It slammed into the dock a few times. Stopped. Slammed some more.

"Been waitin' for ya," a man's voice echoed through the shelter. "Thought ya might've gotten eaten by that shark." A heavy sigh. "There I go with that wishful thinkin' again."

The voice had an almost Texan drawl about it. Like Brax's only deeper and more pronounced. Reminded Cujo a lot of the actor Matthew McConaughey. The clap of cowboy boots on the textured floor of the shelter. Slow. Purposeful.

"Whatcha got in that bag, Cujo?" A chuckle. "Your team is dead, Captain. The Cryptid Force Six program is over."

Cujo frowned while he pulled one of the guns out of the bag, which happened to be a forty-five-caliber pistol. Standard. But it would do the job. Fully loaded. He snatched an extra magazine anyway and stuffed it in his pocket.

"Never thought I'd see the day," the man with the Texan drawl said, "when I'd get the opportunity to meet the one and only Captain Arron Wright. Cujo himself." Very close now. Maybe five feet behind Cujo.

Back still facing the man, Cujo's hand tightened around the pistol's grip. "Who paid you?"

Another chuckle, but the man did not answer.

Rage burst through Cujo. If it was true the assholes killed his team...his vision took on a foggy, almost red hue.

He swallowed and the red retreated a bit. "You're going to kill me anyway. Who paid you?"

A long pause followed.

More footsteps entered the shelter. Some soft. Some loud.

"Someone you shouldn't have fucked with," a familiar voice spoke through a couple of speakers in the shelter.

Cujo's eyes widened. "No."

A scattering of laughter.

Once it quieted, the familiar voice said, "I told you I'd have your asses for what you did to me. Do you really think I'm not a woman of my word?"

"General Kyle," Cujo said, trying to think of a way out of the situation. There was only one exit and that was the door in the far back. "You're supposed to be in prison."

Her snicker through the speakers was unnerving. The evil in it made his blood run cold.

"I am, Captain. But you see…being a General and having *very* special friends in the right places has its perks. My home is half a cell block. Not even dons or drug lords get that much."

"Comparing yourself to the mob or Cartel," Cujo said. "Tell me you're evil without telling me you're evil."

A length of silence. Nothing but the water lapping at the boat.

"Do you know why I haven't had you killed yet, Captain?"

He didn't respond. He stared at the back of the shelter door. How far would he make it before the General's goons opened fire? Would there be someone guarding the door, just in case? How truly organized were the mercenaries General Kyle hired? How experienced were they?

Don't underestimate them. His index finger slipped over the trigger of the pistol.

"Well?" General Kyle said.

"Because you miss my winning personality?"

"I'm sorry, Captain, was that supposed to be a joke?"

"It sounded funny in my head, anyway."

"Last we spoke, Captain, you were well reserved."

Cujo snorted. "Well, a lot has happened between then and now."

A heavy sigh blew out of the speakers. "You're not dead because I have a use for you."

"Uh…look, General…I'm sure you're great and all but I don't think you're my type. I mean—"

"Shut up." Another sigh. "And you call yourself a soldier…"

"I stopped thinking that way a while ago. It's just me and the team now."

"I want you to help me kill Braxton Miller and the Devil Divers."

Cujo frowned and looked at the nearest speaker. "Why?"

"No questions," Kyle snapped. "I have a new team ready for deployment and I want you to lead them."

"You want me to lead a team of…murderers?"

"If you want to call it that." He imagined her waving a liver-spotted hand in a dismissive gesture. Like an evil queen. "I prefer to call it exterminating pests."

"Pests? What did they do to you?"

"I said no questions."

"Fuck you. If you want me to work for you, I need more intel."

"How *dare...*" She cleared her throat. "Fine. I will just say the monster business is quite lucrative these days."

It dawned on him slowly. "You...want to eliminate the competition and build a team of your own. The *only* team."

"Oh, I suppose I might have a couple of teams, so my reach is more global."

"You're insane," Cujo said.

"Maybe, Captain. Maybe. But I'll have more power than the President and be wealthier than the wealthiest." She chuckled. "So, Captain, what do you say? I'll even let you lead my Alpha Team once Mr. Miller is dispatched and his tech in my possession. Better than dead, right?"

"Wrong," Cujo said, as he rolled and took out a short bald man.

Blood splattered the guy standing next to the bald man. A blond guy wearing a bright Hawaiian shirt. Blond Guy grimaced and wiped the blood from the side of his face. The blood smeared, turning that side of the man's gaunt face ghoulish.

"Well, now," Blond Guy said. That heavy Texas drawl. "That ain't very polite."

"What's happening?" General Kyle shouted through the speaker system. "Was that gunfire?"

"Your boy here," Blond Guy said. "He blew half of Marcus's head off."

"Goddamn it, Captain," Kyle said, voice cracking a bit. "Stand down!"

Cujo chuckled and stood. He kept the pistol on Blond Guy. There were others gathering into the shelter now. He counted about a dozen men in all and glanced behind him to make sure the rear exit was clear. How all those men got on the charter boat, Cujo didn't know.

He focused on the men moving closer and closer toward him.

"You just killed one of your teammates," General Kyle said. "You know how much it will cost to find a Marine of that caliber?"

Cujo grunted. "Call it forty-five."

"Marcus was a good Christian," Blond Guy spouted. "He kicked more ass than you ever will, *Captain* Wright."

"A good Christian, huh?" Cujo said, aiming the pistol on Blond Guy's forehead. "How many people did he kill overseas? How many *children*?"

A frown creased the Blond Guy's face.

"Did he think he was doing God's work?"

Blond Guy lifted his pistol and Cujo squeezed the trigger. The back of the man's head blew out in a splash of blood, bone, and brains. It splattered three of the nearest men, who quickly recoiled. One of them screamed when he pulled a chunk of Blond Guy's brain from his hair.

Cujo slowly swept the pistol back and forth. "If you all want to go home to your families or just go home period, I suggest you back away."

"We didn't think you'd actually rescue us." An older man, about Cujo's age, stepped around one of the men splattered with Blond Guy's brains.

Cujo recognized him immediately. The snarled mane of gray hair. The scraggly gray beard. Ropes of muscles for arms. Wiry...

It was the man Cujo left sleeping on his bed. One of the rescues from the sinking charter. His assumption had been right. It was in the plan. A plan General Kyle created and implemented.

The man chuckled. "Look like ya seen a ghost, ol'Hoss."

"Nope," Cujo said. "Just another piece of shit who got people killed."

He pumped two bullets into the man's chest and glanced at the others. "There should be rafts aboard this boat. If you want to live—"

A dull thump sounded from below and the boat rocked just enough to throw Cujo off balance a bit.

"The fuck was that?" one of the men said.

"Captain," General Kyle said through the speakers. "Looks like you didn't—"

"Cujo," Reece cut in. "It's under the boat. Get your suit on! We figured out what was interfering with our comms. Some good hacking."

"It was General Kyle and her goons," Cujo said, still pointing his gun at the other men. "This was all a setup. It was *planned*. All of it."

"Shit," Reece said. "Why aren't you getting into your suit? Are the others there? I'm reading...um...you're in trouble, aren't you?"

"Nothing I can't handle. I'd prefer if they made the right choice, though." His gaze drifted over each man. "Before you do," Cujo added, "where is my team?"

One of the men chuckled, hand slipping to the butt of his sidearm holstered on his hip.

Cujo blew half his face off and turned to the rest. "No time for bullshit. Either I kill you all right now, or you tell me what I need to know. Final warning."

All except for one looked to the floor.

"Cujo," Reece said. "It's circling the boat. Whatever you're going to do you better do it now."

"Well?" he asked the men, attention fully on the one who didn't look down.

A broad shouldered, muscular man with bronze skin and deep, brown eyes.

Finally, the man sighed. "Look, we were supposed to tell you they're dead, so you'd come with us easier."

"Goddamn it, Carl," another man said.

"Shut up," Cujo said to the other man. To Carl, he nodded. "What are you saying?"

"They're still alive. Tied up in the kitchen."

Relief crashed through him in a massive wave so strong his knees about buckled.

"The General is gonna kill you for that, Carl," a man closer to the opening said.

Carl shrugged. "We're going to die anyway. You think we can outrun that fuckin' shark in rafts? We're fucked either way."

"I have an extra one of these suits you can use." Cujo hated himself for even mentioning it because he already missed Ellen, but the man deserved something.

Carl glanced at the suit nearest him and snorted. "My luck I'd hit the self-destruct button."

"I can tell you the commands as we go," Cujo said.

"Oh, fuck this," a man wearing a black baseball cap spouted and lifted an M4.

Cujo ducked behind one of the docks containing a dive suit just as a spray of bullets struck it. Carl leaped, rolled and joined Cujo. He held up a Desert Eagle and gave Cujo a nod. Cujo nodded back.

Carl crouched to the left of the dock, while Cujo crouched on the right.

"Now," Cujo whispered and leaned far enough to pick off one of the men while Carl fired three times.

"Got a couple," Carl said.

"Where's M4?"

Carl shook his head. "Didn't see him."

"You go low," Cujo said. "I'll go high." Which meant he'd have his head fully exposed over the top of the dock. He didn't like the idea but the element of surprise was crucial.

As a duo, they took out three more.

Blood pooled the floor, streaming back and forth gradually with the slight rocking of the boat.

The rest of the men fled. One slipped in a smear of blood, cried out, scrambled to his feet and fell again. In any other circumstance it might have been funny. Not now, though. Finally, the guy gained his feet and ran out of the shelter. He disappeared around the corner.

"They'll try to operate the boat before using the rafts," Carl said.

"Figured so," Cujo said, and slid a fresh mag into the pistol. He nodded at Carl's Desert Eagle. "Got enough mags for that?"

Carl patted the right pocket of his cargo pants. "Three more."

"Good. You take out or subdue the rest of them. I'm getting my team—"

Something heavy thumped against the side of the boat hard enough to send both men into the far wall. Cujo was sure the boat would flip over, but it didn't. Instead, it crashed back down, jarring his guts a bit. Heart stumbling over itself, Cujo got to his feet and ran out of the shelter.

He needed to get to his team before the Black Demon destroyed the boat.

TWENTY-SIX

Cujo opened the door to the living quarters and quickly descended the narrow stairs—

He fell backward just in time to miss a frying pan to the face.

"Get the fucks," Benny shouted.

"It's me," Cujo shouted, not realizing until the last second a knife blade pressed against his throat.

"Pops?" Maze lifted the knife and backed away.

"Holy shit," Benny said as Cujo stood and entered the kitchen. "We thought you were dead."

"Likewise," Cujo said.

A massive shift of the boat knocked them all off their feet.

"You all need to get in your suits now. Its strikes are getting harder. It's testing the boat to see how to attack. You don't have much time."

Cujo nodded at his team. "Let's end this."

While the team rushed to their suits in the shelter, Cujo burst into the wheelhouse to find several men dead, only three remaining and Mary at gunpoint against the far wall by Carl.

When Mary saw Cujo, she blurted a wave of Spanish at him. He only understood a few words here and there. She was talking too fast for him to piece together what she was saying. She had a black eye and the left corner of her mouth oozed blood.

"You hit her?" Cujo asked Carl.

Carl shot a frown at him. "The fuck? No. She was like this when I got here. She had that black eye after we boarded."

"Boarded?"

Carl nodded. "Once your comms and location were hacked, they airlifted the rest of us aboard."

Mary, eyes frantic, flung more Spanish at him.

It made Cujo miss Ellen even more.

"What's all this about her brother?" Carl asked.

Cujo blinked. "You know Spanish?"

He pointed his pistol at the three men semi-conscious on the floor and smiled at Cujo. "My mom is Mexican."

"No shit?" Cujo said and nodded at Mary. "She's talking about her brother?"

"Yeah. Something about he wasn't with the survivors. She keeps asking where her brother is."

Cujo sighed. "Tell her we didn't find him and we're sorry for her loss."

Carl relayed this to Mary in Spanish.

Her bruised face crumpled in a sob while her knees slowly unhinged, and she lowered to the floor.

"Tell her to come with us and we'll get her a lifejacket and a raft, just in case. We need to *move*."

Carl nodded, and relayed the message to Mary. She nodded, though vaguely. She needed the closure, he supposed. Hurt to see all the hurt. It never got any easier.

Cujo turned, found some rope and tied the three groaning men to one of the pipes running along the back wall of the wheelhouse.

"How'd you knock them out like that?" Cujo asked while all three of them vacated the wheelhouse.

Carl chuckled. "Wasn't me." He pointed at Mary running alongside them. "She's a badass."

Cujo smiled.

At the shelter where the team was already in their suits, Cujo and Carl gave Mary a lifejacket and an inflatable raft. Even though, if they failed, the Black Demon would be sure to eat her anyw—

This time when the Black Demon struck the boat it lifted into the air. Loud crunching filled Cujo's ears. Not a sound one wanted to hear on a boat in the Pacific Ocean, hundreds of miles from land.

The force of it flung Cujo, Carl, and Mary in different directions. Cujo's suit, which hadn't been in a dock, was the only thing which remained stagnant. Apparently, it stabilized itself even out of water, Cujo noted while he climbed over empty docks, rucksacks and bags and other supplies. The rest of the team in their suits, also stabilized, helped clear the way for him.

"Carl," Cujo said and pointed at the remaining suit still in its dock. "Go to that and tell it to open."

Carl didn't say anything, which was good. It meant he was following orders.

Mary shouted things in Spanish.

"She says she doesn't know what to do," Carl said as he approached Ellen's suit.

"Open," Cujo commanded his suit and it split open. "I think the shark put a hole in the boat. It might be sinking. Tell her to get as much water and food as she can after we leave. Pull the string to the raft when the boat begins to sink and put all the food and water in it. If there are oars, tell her to grab one or two of those so she can paddle away from here."

Cujo turned, back to the suit. Carl followed his lead. "Tell her we're her vengeance."

Carl looked at the distraught, hurt Mary and told her everything Cujo said in Spanish. She stared at Carl for a long time, then looked at Cujo. A tear rolled down her bruised cheek, and she nodded. She hurried out of the shelter.

"Just walk backward into the suit," Cujo said. "It'll close around and feel weird until everything adjusts to you. Don't freak out. We're all able to communicate with each other so I'll guide you as best I can."

"Okay," Carl said. He closed his eyes and stepped backward into the suit.

Cujo waited for it to close around him before doing the same.

The same sense of being crushed gripped him for a few seconds but dissipated quickly as the suit came online. Hisses and whirs filled the helmet.

A beep and—

"—get off the goddamn boat!"

Cujo blinked. "What's happening?"

"Reece says the big bastard is gonna destroy the boat and to get off it," Benny said. "She's been saying this for like five minutes while you and whoever that is were talking to the woman who probably killed Ellen."

"My name's Carl. And she didn't kill that woman. Marcus did. He got off on that kind of thing, I guess."

"Who the fuck is Marcus?" Maze said. "And where can I find him so I can return the fucking favor?" There was a genuine pain in her voice. She loved Ellen. No question.

"He's dead," Cujo said. "I'll give you details later. Focus on the mission."

"And what's the mission?" Luna said. "Because everything we've tried hasn't worked."

"Was that really General Kyle over the speakers earlier?" Wade said.

"Yes, Wade," Cujo said. "It was her. We'll deal with her later. Luna, just—"

Through the visor of the suit, Cujo watched the floor of the shelter splinter upward. Water sprayed in every direction. Not quite a flood, but...

"Guns," Cujo said, heart thrumming. "The ones we brought for underwater engagement. We use those this time around. Hit it with everything we got." He paused, remembering how it could heal. "We need to completely sever the tail and head from the body. Annihilate the head. It can regenerate."

"What?" Benny said. "Are you fuckin' kidding me?"

"No. It can heal itself. That's why it has lived so long, I think."

"Are you serious?" Reece spouted.

"Yes," Cujo said. "I cut through its gills to escape, and it made sure I saw the gills heal. I about cut its lower jaw off. It sank. Yet here it is again." He watched the water filling the shelter and the slight tilt toward the rear of the boat. "Sever the tail. Destroy the head. That's all I can think of and that might not even work."

No one said anything for a minute or so.

"Try it," Ross said. "If that does not work, I want all of you to use those suits and get the hell out of there."

Cujo, knowing what the Black Demon was capable of, figured there would be two outcomes and he said as much.

"We can run, sure. But it will hunt us. It'll kill all but one, so its story won't be forgotten. Or it'll just fucking eat us all and be done with it. The thing is unpredictable. Get your guns."

He found his AC-900, water edition, and made sure he could use it while in the suit. Trigger guard made everything a bit tight, but nothing he couldn't work with. The suit's fingers were about five times larger than his own.

The others, moving like molasses in the suits, gathered their guns. All except for one.

Carl. He stood in the dock, silent.

Cujo found Ellen's bag but the only thing he found was something resembling a modified crossbow. Instead of everything being open, however, it was all enclosed in matte black.

Frowning, Cujo said, "Reece?"

"You *need* to get out of there, Cujo! It's—"

"It'll do what it'll do. What was Ellen's preferred weapon?"

A pause. "For this mission she chose a prototype." Reece fell silent for a couple of seconds. "It doesn't have a name. Number 66-6 is what Ross says. It's like a hyper powered crossbow. The bolts it shoots are subnuclear."

"What the fuck?" Benny said. "*Seriously?*"

"Ross didn't want her to take it on this mission, but Ellen wanted to try it out."

Cujo grunted. "It's like she knew we'd need something more powerful."

"She was always thinking ahead," Maze said and fell silent again.

Cujo gave the 66-6 to Carl along with something that appeared to be a quiver, though, it too, was a solid thing.

"How the hell do you get the bolts out?" Cujo asked, motioning for Carl to move out of the shelter.

Carl, as fast as the suit would allow, which was like watching a movie in slow motion, made his way toward the opening.

The rest of the team was already waiting for him, but Cujo took another moment for Ellen to respond.

"Ross says it works like a magazine," Reece said, as though on cue. "Once the current one is empty, replace it with a fresh one. This is located at the back of the 66-6 model."

"How many bolts in a mag?" Cujo asked.

A pause, then Ross came on. "Ten. This prototype is extremely new, Cujo. Whoever is going to use it needs to know the risks."

Cujo stepped around the splintered floor. Water sprayed his visor, blinding him for a couple of seconds.

"What are the risks?"

Ross took a few more seconds to respond. "It is possible for a bolt to get lodged in the barrel and explode, killing the owner, everyone and anything within six city blocks."

The boat shook and the suit stabilized itself.

"The boat is breaking in half," Reece said, sounding defeated and tired.

"That's one of three issues," Ross said.

"Carl," Cujo said. "Raise your hand."

A Devil 1 suit raised its hand near the rear of the charter boat.

Cujo went to him and handed the quiver, or, rather, the magazine over. "You heard Ross, right? About how many rounds are in a mag?"

"Ten," Carl said. "Mini sub-nuclear bolts." He sighed. "Not sure about this, though."

"It's all we got," Cujo said. "Without it, you'll be reduced to using the suit's laser and twelve mini-missiles, which don't do shit to this thing."

A loud crash and the rear of the boat dropped.

Cujo used the rearview on the back of the suit just as the Black Demon's head blasted through the boat like a giant harpoon. It thrashed and broke the boat in half.

"Holy shit," Benny shouted.

"Get in the water," Cujo said. The rearview image blinked out of existence and he gaped through the front visor again.

"Not like we have much choice," Maze said. "Boat is sinking."

"Carl," Cujo said, turning to the man in the suit holding the 66-6 crossbow. "Stay close to me. Once in the water, the suit will stabilize itself so just stay put."

"Yes, Sir."

"Call me Cujo. None of that 'Sir' shit in this team."

"Yeah," Benny said. "He prefers to be called Ma'am."

"Shup up," Cujo said.

Benny chuckled.

Cujo waited for the team to jump into the ocean. To Carl, he said, "Go ahead. I'm right behind you."

A shuddery breath sounded. A long exhale. "Okay…okay."

Cujo gave him a shove too quick for the suit's stabilizers to take hold. Carl screamed the entire five feet to the water.

He was still screaming when Cujo joined him.

TWENTY-SEVEN

"Basic functions," Cujo said while the team gathered. He faced Carl. Only way he knew it was Carl was because of the 66-6 crossbow. The guy still held onto it, despite the surprise plunge into the blue ocean water. "Forward, backward, right, left. Dive and surface replace up and down. You can say up and it will listen, though only for six feet increments. With me so far?"

"Uh—"

"Good," Cujo continued. "Speeds. You have low boost, medium boost, and high boost. There's also hyper boost if you need to get—"

"LARGE LIFEFORM DETECTED. TWENTY METERS SOUTH."

"Wh-What was that?" Carl asked.

"God," Benny said. "He works for us now."

"Shut up, Benny."

"Eat butt worms, Captain Cujo, Ma'am."

"You first," Cujo said. "Got them from your mom."

"Y—I...ew, dude."

Cujo rolled his eyes and returned his attention to Carl. "That's the suit's detection sensors. They're all over the suits. A warning system. With any luck, though, you won't have to use the suit much. You're going to be our sniper."

"*Hey,*" Benny said. "That's *my* job."

"Yep," Cujo said. "I want you and Carl to partner up. Benny, you distract the Black Demon to set Carl up with good shots to the head. The rest of us will be working on the tail."

"Now I'm a spotter. Demoted." Benny sighed. Absolute theatrics. "Thanks, new guy. Dick."

"I'm sorry, I didn't—"

"Pay no attention to that buffoon," Cujo said. "You've heard of the class clown? Benny here is the team clown." Cujo paused for effect. "And he knows better than to clown around during a mission."

Benny snorted. "Sorry, Boss. Carl, dude, please forgive me."

Carl was quiet for a few seconds then chuckled. "This has to be the weirdest team I've ever come across. Y'all are craz—"

"LARGE LIFEFORM DECETED. FIFTEEN METERS SOUTH AND CLOSING."

"You two stay here," Cujo said. "Benny, you know the distances needed to do what has to be done, right?"

"Not really," Benny said. "But I'll figure it out."

"Good. Luna, Maze, Wade and I will be trying to distract it enough to stay in the same area. Our target is the tail. Everyone understand the mission?"

A volley of yeses poured through his helmet speakers.

"Good. Let's bag us a demon shark."

Cujo, Maze, Luna and Wade high boosted toward the Black Demon while Benny and Carl were left in a wake of bubbles.

"Okay, man," Benny said through Cujo's suit speakers. "We need to get about fifty feet apart."

"I'm not sure I can do this," Carl said.

"Sure you can. Listen, I know it's an evil, massive, murderous cryptid shark that shouldn't exist, but that doesn't make it immortal." A pause. "Or maybe it does. I dunno. If not, hell, there are worse ways to die, right?"

Carl didn't say anything and Cujo rolled his eyes. *God, you suck at motivational speeches, Benny.*

"Okay, fifty feet apart. I'll shoot in various spots to keep it in profile position. Then you aim that weird crossbow thingy at Big Boy's eye. Easiest access point to the brain. But if those are sub-nuclear, I'm not sure you really have to worry about a kill shot."

"So…just shoot the fucker, then?"

A slight pause from Benny. A snort. "Now you're gettin' it, New Guy!"

"Carl."

"Oh, yeah. Sorry, man. New Guy Carl!"

Carl sighed and Cujo smiled. He knew that sigh well. He had issued it more times than he could count working with Benny over the years.

"LARGE LIFEFORM DETECTED. TWENTY METERS DIRECTLY BELOW."

"Shit," Maze said. "How'd it get underneath without us detecting it? Or…hey, where the hell is Reece?"

Everyone transitioned in speeds to slow. Then they set their suits to tread.

"Reece?" Cujo said. "You there?"

Silence.

"What the fuck now?" Benny said.

"You just get in position," Cujo said. "Shit's about to hit the fan."

"Yes, Boss."

"Reece?"

Still, nothing but infinite silence.

"Something's wrong at HQ," Maze said.

"You think the General…" Luna trailed off.

Cujo's heart sank. He didn't want to think of what could be happening at HQ. Didn't want to know what General Kyle had up her sleeve. So, for the time being, he focused solely on the Black Demon.

One monster at a time…

"Our sensors haven't gone off," he said, trying to redirect everyone's attention back to the immediate threat. "Must just be sitting down there."

"Why?" Wade asked. "I don't get it."

"Because it likes playing its games," Cujo said. "We're going to need to be creative and quick witted. It's a cunning bastard, but we can do better. We do not split up this time. One force. All we got. Let's send this fucker back to Hell."

"Fuckin' A, Pops," Maze said.

"We dive at high boost under it and shoot until it moves in Benny and Carl's direction."

"It's like wrangling a bull, or something," Wade muttered.

"More like prodding it to where we want it to go."

"Let's do it," Luna said. "All or nothing."

"All or nothing," Cujo said and added, "Dive."

TWENTY-EIGHT

Do or die.

One final time.

All…or nothing.

Words. Always mere words until action forced the words to happen. Sometimes it worked, sometimes it failed.

At five hundred feet below the surface of the ocean, Cujo understood the power of words and action together. He knew it like he knew his favorite sandwich is a bologna, ham, mayo and mustard conglomeration topped with Swiss cheese.

Without action, words were pointless things during a fight or battle. War. Words without action became moot things. Here and gone, swept away by bitter winds.

All four of the team slipped by the Black Demon without it noticing. Or at least Cujo hoped it hadn't noticed. They were about sixty feet under it when he told Luna, Maze, and Wade to stop.

"I don't think it saw us," Cujo said. "Let's get within range and poke this monster toward Benny and Carl. Once in position, we attack the tail. Sever it. Destroy it. Obliterate the fucking thing. All we got. But remember, only when we're in Benny and Carl's area of engagement."

"Yeah," Benny said. "Don't ruin the fun for us and, like, kill the bastard or anything good like that before you get it to us. Hashtag, hard eyeroll."

Cujo shook his head and didn't respond to Benny.

"LARGE LIFEFORM DETECTED. ONE-HUNDRED-AND-SIXTY FEET ABOVE. MOVING EAST AT TWENTY MILES PER HOUR."

"It's moving away from us," Luna said.

"We're northwest," Benny said.

"Did it give up, you think?" Maze said.

Cujo turned until he faced east. "No. It's fucking with us."

"I thought it didn't see us—"

Cujo cut Wade off. "I don't think it did, but it sensed us, somehow." He hated not having Reece shooting him facts into his ear. Without her, he was winging it. He hated winging anything. There needed to be some form of structure. A way to…

"Follow it," Cujo said, not really sure if the decision was good or bad. A gut feeling. Another thing he despised, though went with on more than one occasion over the years. Sometimes the gut was right. Sometimes…

"It wants us to try and circle around and face it, but, if we follow it, staying in its wake and maintaining the one hundred feet advantage, we might be able to poke the thing back in the direction we need it to be."

"I dunno," Maze said.

"Yeah," Benny said. "Sounds fishy."

A collective groan from the team. Cujo rolled his eyes.

"I think it'll work," Cujo said. "C'mon."

He went into high boost following the Black Demon. Soon enough, the other three joined him.

"LARGE LIFEFORM DETECTED. ONE-HUNDRED-FORTY FEET ABOVE. IN PURSUIT. FORTY METERS AND CLOSING."

"I don't know about this," Wade said.

"Just remain within range of your weapon and shoot it if it turns away from the direction, we need it to go," Cujo said.

"I don't know," Wade said. "I have a bad feeling."

"Probably all those burritos," Benny said.

"No," Wade said, not even sounding irritated, which probably got under Benny's skin a bit, Cujo figured. Benny liked to know if he got to someone or not. "Not the burritos. Just…I don't know…"

"Well, stow it for now," Cujo said. "Let's get this big bastard swung around toward Benny and Carl."

Everyone fell silent. Only the gurgling rush of the water around the suit and their own breathing. Something which still unnerved Cujo. You're never really aware of your breathing until you are. And, sometimes, it's a jarring thing.

The sensation faded quickly, however, as they neared the creature.

"LARGE LIFEFORM DETECTED. FIFTY—" The suit's monotone voice cut off and fell silent for a couple of seconds. "LIFEFORM DETECTED. ONE HUNDRED FEET AND CLOSING."

"The fuck?" Maze said.

"It turned around," Luna said.

"Told you I had a bad feeling," Wade said.

Mind reeling, Cujo finally came up with an alternate plan. "Dive another one hundred feet. The suits can withstand one thousand, remember. Should be about nine hundred."

"Then what?" Luna asked.

"Then we wait until it's directly above us, high boost until we're all within range, and shoot the hell out of it until it decides to run into Benny and Carl."

"I will have Benny and the new guy pinged for you," Reece said out of nowhere. "Password is triple protected. It's all I can do right now."

Cujo frowned. "What's going on? Everything okay there?"

Static.

He clenched his jaw, waited a couple of seconds, and said, "Okay." The pings of Benny and Carl popped up on the helmet's visor. Top right. "You all see Benny and Carl?"

They said they did.

"Good. Follow the plan and if shit goes wrong, we'll just have to play it by ear."

No one said anything, nor did they have to. The danger was clear enough. If they fucked up, there wasn't much of a plan B, or really playing it by ear. The creature would eat them all. Surely, it was getting bored and hungry by now.

Cujo assumed its game now was to get them close, lure them in, so to speak, and annihilate them so it could go about its life for another fifty or one hundred years without anyone bothering it but its legend growing stronger.

The message was clear. It didn't like being messed with. However, it liked the publicity. Or something like that. Every attack, it left one person alive to tell the tale. At least, that's how it seemed. Unless that many people were just lucky...

"LARGE LIFEFORM DETECTED. DIRECTLY ABOVE. EIGHTY FEET."

"This is it," Cujo said. "Benny and Carl are southwest of us. We need to push the fucker in that direction. You all got that?"

"Yep," Luna said.

"Yeah, Pops," Maze said.

"Oo-rah," Wade said.

All four boosted on medium to the northeast side of the Black Demon. A tricky stunt, trying to stay out of the shark's vision or sensory glands. If it caught wind they were there, Cujo knew it would all be over.

Cujo checked Reece's pings on Benny and Carl. Both were still in the same position. But...

"We need to bump it up another sixty feet or so," he said. "Luna, use that cannon of yours to give this beast a shove upward."

"On it," Luna said and darted under the shark.

"On my mark," Cujo said. He waited for Luna to take position with her water version of the M32A1 grenade launcher. He just hoped the grenades were impact and not delayed. He aimed his AC-900 at the side of the shark while pacing its casual glide. "Now."

Luna fired a grenade at the underside of the Black Demon. The grenade exploded on impact between the pectoral fins. Chest area. Whatever. Cujo wasn't sure what that spot was called on a shark.

Nonetheless, the creature thrashed. Its long tail whipped in Cujo, Maze and Wade's direction.

"Don't let the tail hit you," Cujo shouted. "Down boost high."

He shot downward before the tail crashed into him, not sure if the others had done the same or not yet because he collided with something. Spinning, tumbling head over feet until the suit stabilized.

"Something hit me," Luna said. "Don't know what it was."

"Probably me," Cujo said, waiting for his equilibrium to return a bit. "Maze? Wade?"

"Here," Maze said. "Didn't have time to follow but we backed away far enough to miss the tail. Its force, or whatever, sent us farther out, though. We're on our way back."

"Good. Can you see if it's heading toward the surface?"

"No. After all that, I lost track of it."

"Shit. Benny, keep an eye out. Not sure what this thing will do now."

"Oh, joy," Benny said.

"The rest of us," Cujo said, "let's find it. The mission isn't over."

Once Maze and Wade joined Luna and Cujo, they set out in search of the Black Demon.

Can't lose track of it, Cujo thought. *It can't get the upper hand.*

But the more they searched and found nothing but sea turtles, a few sharks and various fish, the more Cujo's hopes sank like the remains of the boat they all came in. Long lost in the darkness. It—

"LARGE LIFEFORM DETECTED. SOUTH, SIXTY METERS. DEPTH: ONE HUNDRED FEET."

"You all got that," he said. "Head south. Hyper boost to twenty meters. Remember, you can't steer during hyper, so try to aim correctly."

"Oh," Maze said. "This sounds like death waiting to happen. Go team!" She chuckled humorlessly.

Cujo smiled and positioned himself due south. "Together."

"Together," the other three repeated.

"Hyper boost," Cujo said, and barely managed to blink before he was blasting through the water at a speed he didn't even want to comprehend.

TWENTY-NINE

"LARGE LIFEFORM DETECTED. SOUTH, FORTY METERS AND CLOSING. DEPTH: ONE HUNDRED FEET."

"We need to give it a nudge west," Cujo said, eying the locations of Benny and Carl. "Ten degrees at least."

Cujo, Luna, Maze and Wade made their way to the east side of the Black Demon. Such a massive creature, Cujo reflected, though beautiful in its own murderous way. This titan of the deep. This thing that should not be. It had survived for decades, somehow. Maybe even centuries. Yes, it was beautiful. Strange and terrifying. A true force to be reckoned with. A shark that size, how could it elude experts for so long? He wondered how many more massive mysteries awaited discovery in the deepest, most remote areas of any ocean. What other horrors lurked in the depths?

"Okay," Cujo said once they were all in position. "Let's give him that nudge."

They fired their weapons at the same time, all striking the monster just above and around the right pectoral fin.

The Black Demon's tail lashed so fast, none of them had time to move. It crashed into them and sent them tumbling. Cujo tried commanding the suit to stabilize, but the impact did something to his suit. The words blinking on the visor told him: CANNOT COMPUTE COMMAND. PLEASE STAND BY. So, instead of stabilizing, he continued to tumble through the water at a speed he didn't even want to think about.

Maze, Luna and Wade all cried out at some point but the madness he was stuck in took precedence.

"Stabilize," Cujo shouted.

He continued to tumble. Head over feet, spiraling out of control, farther and farther away from the Black Demon and for all he knew, his team. The suit wouldn't comply and except for life support he was on his own unless the suit finally woke up.

The monster's tail strike broke it. Or so it seemed. Cujo frowned as all the words lit up in red on the helmet's visor. 'Damage' was the largest and the one his sight lingered on longer than the rest. What kind of damage? Possible leak? Was the force was strong enough to knock out relays to the suit's command center?

Damage…

"Stabilize," he roared.

And, for a wonder, the spinning slowed to a stop and he gaped through all the red words, through the visor and directly into the open maw of the Black Demon.

"Dive," he shouted. "Hyper boost!"

The suit beeped; didn't move.

"Dive! Hyper boost!"

The suit didn't move.

His world soon became the toothy cavern he remembered from getting eaten before and—

The suit beeped again, bent and dove into the deeper darkness. "High boost." He needed to try and slow it gradually. An abrupt stop would not only hurt him, but probably leave the suit incapacitated. "Medium boost."

Cujo's suit slowed...slowed.

"Slow boost."

Barely moving, he said, "Stop."

The suit stopped, but his heart hammered, striking nerves. His breathing was erratic and shallow. The suit told him to try and relax. It told him about a pressure warning. It detected a larger lifeform twenty meters above. Like all that was supposed to help calm his terrified ass. He knew then what he knew before. He hated the suit. Hated all of its cold, inhuman words. Its monotone voice. Its—

"Pops? You there? Hello? Wade? Luna? For fuck sake...*Benny*?"

"Here," Cujo managed.

"Thank God," Maze said, sounding like a mother seeing her child breathe again after nearly drowning to death. "Thought I lost all of you there for a second."

"So did I," Luna said. "I see someone. Not sure who. On your six."

"Hey," Wade said. He sounded as weary as Cujo felt.

"Luna, Wade. What depth are you at?"

"Three-hundred-and-forty-two feet," Luna said.

Cujo checked his depth and blinked. "Damn. I'm just below six hundred."

"Jesus Christ, Pops," Maze said. "How'd you end up there?"

"Hell if I know," he said. "Any of you see where the Black Demon went?"

A long pause.

"Uh," Benny said. "Yeah, so...it's here. It's looking right at me, Boss. Ugly giant thing, isn't it?"

"Follow through with the mission," Cujo said. "The kill shot is coming from Carl. Keep it focused on you, Benny!"

"Ya know, this vacation really sucks, right?"

"If we live through this," Cujo said, "we'll go on another one."

"Uh-huh. Do you ever shut up, Boss? I'm trying to focus here."

Cujo smiled and joined the other three. "We will keep our distance and offer support if it decides to run."

"Shut the fuck up, Boss," Benny said.

Cujo opened his mouth and closed it. Benny was the sniper. Benny knew what to do. Benny *knew* when to be quiet while working. It was just the other ninety-eight percent of the time he didn't shut up.

"It's turning away," Benny whispered. "Gonna pluck the fucker back in line. Carl, you ready?"

"Yes," Carl said.

"Soon as the bastard turns, blow its fuckin' head off."

"Right," Carl said. "Just worry about getting it in position."

Benny snorted. "Looks like you got another contender for your leadership crown, Boss."

Cujo shook his head. "Stay focused out there. We're on our way."

Luna, Wade, Maze and Cujo high boosted in the direction of the Black Demon and whatever the future held within its massive jaws.

THIRTY

"There," Benny said. "Kill the fucker."

"Okay, just…" Carl said.

"*Shit*," Benny said. "You missed. It's okay. Hold on. We'll get it turned back around. Take your time lining up the shot. Exhale when you pull the trigger and try not to think too much."

"Okay," Carl said.

Cujo listened with a loose smile. He never paid much attention when Benny taught someone. Even it was only digging a hole, Benny was always patient and reassuring. He offered tips and advice rather than berate whoever he trained. He knew there was much more to Benny than the jokes, childish rants, and goofiness, but those often covered up the other traits. Like his patience and knowledge while teaching.

Before Benny got the Black Demon into position, Cujo and the rest of the team slowed to a stop within one hundred feet of it. Not for the first time, Cujo found himself in awe of the monster. It could be a blue whale for all its immense size. Size, yes, though definitely built like a kind of great white/ thresher shark hybrid.

Luna, Wade, Maze and Cujo watched, weapons ready, while Benny strategically popped the Black Demon with bullets, getting the creature to shift into a better position for Carl.

"Hold," Cujo told the rest of his team. "If it tries to run, we wrangle it back here. That's our job right now."

"And if something goes wrong?" Maze asked.

"Then we adjust plans and get it back within range of Carl's crossbow," Cujo said. "Unless one of you wants to get eaten…"

The long string of silence gave him his answer.

"There," Benny said. "Fire!"

A couple of seconds later the head of the Black Demon became a huge cloud of flashing oranges and reds. The force of the blast rocked Cujo and his team, testing the stabilizers. In the end, they were only pushed back a few feet.

"H*ooo*ly shit," Benny said.

"We can't tell from here, Benny," Cujo said. "Direct hit?"

"Yeah, Boss. New Guy got the son of a bitch dead-on. Blew the bastard's head right off."

Red bubbles and chunks of flesh frothed and mixed with the rest as the orange flashes diminished. Soon enough, everything was red. And it was spreading.

"Benny," Cujo said. "We're a little over one hundred feet from you to the north. Our depth is three-hundred-and-two feet. I want you guys over here before all that blood—"

"LARGE LIFEFORM DETECTED. APPROACHING FROM THE NORTH AT UNKNOWN SPEED. ONE HUNDRED METERS AND CLOSING."

Cujo blinked.

"Wait," Maze said. "How the fuck did it get all the way back there so fast?"

"It can't," Benny said. He sounded out of breath. "There's no way. I watched its ugly-ass head explode. I saw it start to *sink*. It can't—"

"There's two of them," Cujo said, eyes widening. His heart thudded heavily. "Benny, you and Carl get your asses over here."

"Oh, this is just fuckin' fantastic," Benny said. "Two? That means we killed a family member and the other one is gonna be *pissed*."

"Just hurry up and get here," Cujo said. "We need to get away from this spot as fast as possible."

Benny and Carl were there within a couple of minutes and, as a team, they high boosted away from the giant blood cloud.

"Carl," Cujo said. "Do you know the range on your weapon?"

"No."

"Just a guess," Benny chimed in, "but I think I would say lethal within one hundred yards."

"Okay." Cujo had them all slow to slow boost. "We're going to double back. Carl, once you reach ninety yards, I want you to stabilize the suit and wait to get a clear shot."

"Sounds good," Carl said. No hesitation. Cujo liked that.

"So, the same plan as before?" Benny said.

"Yep. The three of us will wrangle the thing and steer it toward you two. You nudge it into position and Carl blasts its head off."

Silence drifted through the team and even though they were all in high-tech dive suits, the tension was so thick Cujo could almost see it floating between each person.

"Okay," he said after a moment. "Let's get this done."

Maze, Luna, Wade and Cujo boosted in the direction Carl killed the first Black Demon but...

"Holy shit," Maze said. "You see this, Pops?"

Cujo's mouth opened. His blood turned icy, barely a trickle through his veins. His breathing paused.

The first one had been big, but this...this monstrosity was even larger. If the first was the size of a blue whale, this one was two, maybe even three blue whales. It slowly drifted in a circle. First gliding around the dissipating blood cloud then swimming through it. A couple of minutes of this and it stopped above where the last one sank into the depths.

Its long tail drooped and for a moment, Cujo's heart ached a bit. He watched the titan of a shark actually grieve for its dead kin. He felt its sorrow as if it found its way through the intakes and into the suit.

"Uh, Pops?"

Cujo drew in a breath, and blew it out. "What?"

"Are we gonna, like, wrangle this thing and go home, or just watch it float there for another five minutes?"

"It's sad," Luna said. Her voice was barely above a whisper.

"So what?" Maze said. "If not for this thing we wouldn't be out here right now and El would still be alive."

"It didn't kill Ellen, though," Wade said.

"No shit," Maze said. "Are you not listening, or what? I said if *not* for this thing." A sigh. Maze's tone darkened. "And Mary's father. That son of a bitch will pay."

Cujo let Maze's facts settle and focused on the monstrous shark.

It revealed more emotion than the last one. Did that mean the thing was smarter or was he overthinking? The drooping tail. The way it just floated there as if in mourning. A deep-sea funeral, now that Cujo thought about it.

Finally, Cujo took a shaky breath and said, "Okay. Let's get it into position."

"Were you guys seriously just watching that thing for five minutes?" Benny said.

Letting Benny's comment slide, Cujo said, "Luna, Wade...you go to its right flank. Maze and I will be on the left to turn it around and get it facing Benny and Carl. Give it a nudge anytime it veers away from the objective. Luna, use those grenades as strategically as possible."

"I will," Luna said and, along with Wade, boosted toward the much larger Black Demon.

"I can't believe there's two," Maze said, drifting to Cujo's left.

"Explains why they've been around so long," he said. "They've been breeding."

A pause. "But wouldn't they be family?" Maze sounded baffled.

"Who knows," Cujo said while they moved into position. "I really don't think it matters out here anyway. As long as the bloodline continues."

"Right," Maze said. "You think it knows we're here?"

They drifted into position about eighty feet from the Black Demon's left pectoral fin.

"Probably," Cujo said. "But I don't know. Maybe it doesn't see us as a threat at all and taking its time to mourn? Maybe it just doesn't care? I don't know."

"Okay," Wade said. "We're in position, I think."

"Eighty feet out?" Cujo said.

"Ninety-six," Luna said. "I want to lob a few if Wade's bursts don't steer it right."

Cujo frowned. "No. Get closer. Eighty-five at least. If Wade's rounds don't move the thing then it'll be up to you to get it to move."

"Moving in," Luna said. "I didn't think of that. Thanks, Cujo."

"Yup. Both of you be alert over there. I don't know how this one will react."

"Now at eighty-six feet from the shark," Wade said.

"I'm settling here," Luna said. "Firing in ten...nine...eight..."

Cujo swallowed down a hard lump in his throat and focused all of his attention on the Black Demon. Within eighty feet, some of its size disappeared a bit. Especially the tail. The suit only illuminated so much at this depth. More than without, but Cujo still wished he could see more of the beast. He needed to gauge its movements if and when it moved.

For the time being, however, it remained stagnant over its kin's watery grave.

"...three...two...one..." Luna said.

Cujo lifted his deep-sea AC-900 and waited for whatever shitshow followed.

THIRTY-ONE

The explosions happened within about three seconds of each other, each one smacking the Black Demon's head like a vicious slap.

And yet, it merely turned away from the blasts and didn't leave the spot.

"I…" Luna said. "I don't know why it's not moving."

"I'm shooting it right now, too," Wade said. "There's blood, but it's just not doing anything, Captain."

"Cujo," Cujo said. "I'm not a Captain anymore. Try shooting an eye."

A few seconds of silence streamed out.

"Nothing," Wade said.

"I'm going to get closer and give it another three hits," Luna said. "It's injured. There's blood."

"Keep shooting," Cujo said. "Don't let up until it turns toward us."

"Ten-four," Luna said.

Cujo stared at the Black Demon. He watched tendrils of blood swirl above its head. It didn't move. Not the gills, mouth…nothing. It was like some higher power shut the monster down.

Larger flashes silhouetted the shark. Luna's grenades. Plumes of blood and bits of flesh clouded the water.

And still…the massive Black Demon did not move.

"What the fuck is wrong with it?" Maze said. "That had to hurt like hell."

"What's going on, guys?" Benny said.

"Luna and Wade hit it with multiple rounds," Cujo said.

"I can hear, Boss. Why isn't it moving?"

"I don't know," Cujo said, frowning. "I don't know what—"

The Black Demon's head jerked upward after a fourth blow from Luna. Bubbles, black and red and silvery blew out of the creature's gills in muddy torrents. That final grenade, it was like some ancient awakening. The monster's head swept back and forth for a second or two, then, all at once, its massive body swayed.

At first, it appeared to turn in Cujo and Maze's direction, then stopped. Once again, it fell absolutely still.

Cujo, heart hammering, blew out a breath he didn't know he had been holding.

"I don't get it," Wade said. "Why—"

The Black Demon sprang to life. It shot toward Cujo so fast he didn't have time to react. One second it looked like a statue, the next, its arrow-shaped head glided up to about twenty feet away from Cujo and stopped in profile. An onyx eye the size of a beach ball glared directly at Cujo.

"Oh," Maze said in a shaky voice. "Oh, shit."

It didn't attack, however. No, instead it appeared to be inspecting Cujo. They didn't have any scent inside the suits, but that didn't mean the shark couldn't see them. As with the other, this one could see them just fine.

The monster stared at him, and he stared back.

In a blink, it could chomp him to bits. No doubt it was faster than the dead one. Cujo wouldn't have enough time to dodge the teeth.

He gaped at his reflection in the shiny void of the shark's eye. Yes, as before, Cujo felt if he gazed into that black fathom he'd be sucked in and lost forever. He glanced away.

"Hold on, Pops," Maze whispered. "I'll see if I can—"

"No," Cujo said and closed his eyes for a bit. "Don't move. I think it's trying to see if we were the ones that killed its mate."

"We're the only things here," Luna said. "It must know."

"Everyone just…just standby," Cujo said and opened his eyes.

The second he did, the giant shark slipped by. It didn't hurry. Indeed, it appeared not to care in the least. Just an old monster swimming back out into the depths after its mate was killed. With nothing more to live for, the beast would disappear, and its legend would vanish with it. Before long, no one would remember why they were so terrified of the ocean in this section of the world.

The long tail didn't create enough force to move Cujo and Maze and Cujo couldn't help feeling a little sorry for the creature. A thing that shouldn't exist, but did and was only trying to survive, despite the odd obsession of toying with its prey.

"Damn," Maze said. "Should we…"

"No," Cujo said and sighed. "Let it go. This was a fool's mission anyway."

A few minutes passed.

"So, um," Benny said. "Can we go home now? This vacation sucks fuzzy donkey balls."

Cujo nodded. "Yeah. Let's head back to land. We've done enough here."

He waited until all of his team, including Carl, joined him and Maze. He gave the vast blue of the Pacific one final glance. Lovely, in its own terrifying way. He looked off in the direction the Black Demon swam in and wondered how long the species would go on without a mate. Unless there was another Black Demon out there somewhere, which, in all honesty, Cujo couldn't see why not. The oceans were mysteries for the most part. And whatever swam in its dark depths…swam alone.

He sighed again and said, "Okay. Let's go home."

At high boost, they made their way east.

Cujo wondered about Reece and Ross. What happened at the facility? Were they okay?

One thing was for sure, if either were hurt, especially Reece…whoever did it would pay. He didn't care who it was.

And so, slipping through the water, dodging various forms of sea life, Cujo's mind switched from focusing on the Black Demon to Reece, Ross and the facility.

And General Kyle…

THIRTY-TWO

"MANY LIFEFORMS DETECTED," the suit said, startling Cujo out of his rambling thoughts. "TWO THOUSAND FEET EAST AND CLOSING. POSSIBLE HUMANS."

"The beach," Benny said.

"*A* beach," Maze said. "We might've missed the Baja beach for all we know."

"Without Reece," Cujo said, "it's hard to say. Land is land at this point."

No one argued.

He couldn't wait. Even if they had only been in the ocean for a day or so, the very thought of land being so close made him want to go into hyper boost just to get there faster. He wouldn't miss the vast loneliness of those deep, dark waters. No matter how beautiful it might be. Just to—

"LARGE LIFEFORM DETECTED. APPROACHING FROM THE WEST. EIGHT HUNDRED FEET."

Cujo's breath caught in his throat like a rusty fishhook.

"LARGE LIFEFORM DETECTED. TWENY FEET AND—"

A series of beeps filled the suit. Movement below him.

"Shit," Benny said. "Oh, *shit*."

Not far below them, maybe fifty feet or so, travelling faster than the high boost of their suits, swam a massive shadow. One so large, it could only be one thing.

"The Black Demon," Cujo managed through lips that felt like rubber flaps.

"It tricked us," Maze said.

Cujo blinked, swallowing down a hard lump in his throat. "Goddamn it, I should've known. It was all fake. It wanted us to feel sorry for it. We let it go and now it's..." His eyes widened. "It's heading for the beach." His thoughts jumbled together for a second or two and all he could do was stare at the monster as it swept ahead of them.

"Many lifeforms," Luna said.

"People," Benny said. "Oh, hell, Boss, all those people are—"

"Everyone hyper boost directly for the beach," Cujo said, heart slamming. "Remember, you can't steer so make sure you're pointed in the right direction."

"What about rocks and stuff?" Wade said.

"Gotta take the chance," Cujo said. "Move!"

The Black Demon was nowhere to be seen.

"Hyper boost," he commanded both his suit and his team.

There wasn't any easing into it. Hyper boost in a split second blasted through the water at a speed he didn't even want to think about.

Someone screamed. Someone else cried, "Holy fuck!"

Meanwhile, it took all of Cujo's strength and the suit's aid to hold his head up enough to see where he was going. Which didn't help much anyway. The world became a swirling blur. If there were any large rocks or a shelf, or rise in the sea floor, they wouldn't know it until they crashed into it with so much force it broke open the suits and…

"LARGE LIFEFORM DETECTED," the suit chimed. "ONE THOSAND FEET AHEAD AND CLOSING."

Cujo wished the suits would give an ETA. At least then they could prepare a little.

"LARGE LIFEFORM DETECTED. SIX HUNDRED FEET AND CLOSING."

"Switch to high boost now," Cujo said. "At four hundred feet, downshift to medium boost. At two hundred, low. Unless you want to turn to bloody scrambled eggs then go full stop."

"I mean," Benny said, "you could've just said to step down our speeds before stopping, but I guess the scrambled eggs visual will give me nightmares forever."

"Once we stop, then what, Pops?" Maze said.

"Then we assess the situation and eliminate the threat."

No one protested and, thankfully all went as planned.

Everyone slowed and was drifting into a stop—

"Jesus," Cujo managed while the suit slowed to a stop.

No one said anything and Cujo found himself momentarily paralyzed as body parts, mostly arms and legs from what he could tell, floated and collided in the maelstrom of scarlet water.

The Black Demon rushed by, sending a surge of bloody water and limbs at the team. The suits stabilized. A twitching leg smacked into Cujo then flailed out of sight. A severed head bounced off his chest. The world became a swirling mess. A horror show. Cujo had seen his fair share of carnage throughout the years, but this…this…

His stomach lurched and he fought the urge to puke.

Finally, Benny said, "They're…they're all dead, aren't they? We're too late."

Cujo let go a breath he didn't know he was holding and grimaced while smaller sharks feasted on the smorgasbord of human remains: The bits and pieces the Black Demon left in its wake.

Through red tinted water, he caught a glimpse of the monster. Its belly scraped the sandy floor of the shallows. This didn't appear to worry or harm it any as it continued its gruesome rampage. Not eating. No. Just killing. Killing anything and everything in its path. Among the storm of body parts was other debris like boat propellers, chunks of wood, what Cujo assumed was fiberglass, and God knew what else. The shark was laying waste to *everything*.

"It's punishing us," Cujo said under his breath. "It wants us to hurt like it hurts. It wants us to know loss."

"How do you know that, though?" Benny asked.

Cujo sighed. "I don't. Just…just a gut feeling."

"All those people," Luna said. She sounded on the verge of tears.

Cujo glowered at the Black Demon when it plowed by for a third time. This time south to north. "Carl, you're our kill-shot. I want you within range at all times. Even if we don't present you with an opportunity, I want you to fire if you see an opening. This fucker dies today."

Did he feel sorry for it? Yes. Was he tired of playing games? Yes, to the fifth power.

Enough was enough.

"Listen up," Cujo said. "Give it everything you got. Take out fins, anything to disorientate and incapacitate it enough for Carl. Carl, stay within range of the shark at all times."

"Yes, Sir."

"Call me Cujo."

"Yes, S—Cujo."

"Hate to break up discarding the whole awkward as hell command thing you two are doing," Benny said, "but I have this weird feeling we're, um…being watched."

Cujo frowned, glanced around, then froze.

The churning gore they floated in settled just enough to reveal the Black Demon staring directly at them.

He sucked in a sharp breath as if slapped. His heart stuttered.

"LARGE LIFEFORM DETECTED," the suit said. "ONE HUNDRED FEET EAST. STRAIGHT AHEAD."

Cujo breathed and narrowed his glare on the monster. "Lock and load. Hit it hard."

"Oo-rah," Wade said.

Cujo waited a bit, and lifted his deep-sea modified AC-900. He drew in a breath and roared, "Go, go, go!"

In a split second, they rushed at the Black Demon, guns blazing.

Not a tactic Cujo liked, but maybe, if they took the monster off guard for a minute or two…

Just enough for Carl to get a good shot…

The creature snapped its cavernous jaws shut. Human remains shot out of its gills. Small blooms of blood appeared and dissipated with every bullet the monster took. None of which appeared to have any effect on the thing.

"LARGE LIFEFORM. FIFTY FEET EAST. STRAIGHT AHEAD."

"We're within Carl's range," Cujo shouted. "Split and give him a clear—"

The Black Demon shifted, moved to the right, slipped to the left, then surged directly at them before shooting to the south and disappearing like a bullet.

"The fuck?" Maze said. "Y'all see that?"

"Yup," Cujo said. "Stay alert. It's toying with us. Has been since we saw it." A thought popped up in his head. "This one will try to play more with your emotions, I think. Don't let it get to you. Shoot to kill. If you can't, remember to get it closer to Carl."

"I'm ready," Carl said. "Almost shot when it came at us."

"Oh no you didn't," Benny said. "Head-on like that won't do anything."

"Maybe," Carl said.

"M-*Maybe*?" Benny said. "Dude, who's the fuckin' sniper of this team? What? No answer? That's right, it's me."

Cujo blinked.

Typically, Benny was a very patient teacher. Maybe it was the dire situation they were stuck in. Like the rest of them, Benny was stressed near to capacity. It's all Cujo would allow himself to assume, anyway.

"Stay sharp," Cujo said. "It's playing its game." He glanced around the bloody water. "We're in the shallows. It can still get us, but—"

"Maybe we can beach it," Maze said. "Trick it into chasing us right up onto the beach."

"My thoughts exactly," Cujo said.

"How the hell are we supposed to do that?" Benny said.

Cujo sighed. "I don't know yet."

A few seconds crawled by.

"So," Luna said. "Are we just going to chill here until it comes back?"

No one replied and the question floated like something unwanted between them.

"Look," Carl spoke up, "I'm not sure how this team functions and the lack of military discipline is still messing with me, but I think we should go after it again. The beaching idea feels like a long shot."

As with Luna, no one replied. Well, at least not right away.

Cujo nodded. "So, attack it until either it's dead or we are, correct?"

"Well, not exactly like that, but I think if we can blow its head off like the other one, we have a better chance with that than fucking around trying to beach it, don't you think?"

Cujo grunted. "I don't know what to think, but we'll try your plan." To the rest of the team, he added, "We get our asses to deeper water. My three, we'll do the wrangling thing like before. Benny and Carl, blow its head off."

"Pops," Maze said. "I'm sure this new guy might have some good cred in the Army, or whatever—"

"Sergeant Xavier of the United States Army," Carl said.

"Excuse me, Sergeant Xavier of the United States Army, but what makes you think you have any say in this team? For fuck sake, only a few hours ago you tried to kill us."

Cujo sighed. "She's right, Carl. You're not officially a part of the team."

"I understand, but—"

"LARGE LIFEFORM DETECTED. WEST MOVING EAST. EIGHT HUNDRED FEET AND CLOSING."

"Welp," Benny said. "Looks like we fucked around and found out."

"Head for the beach," Cujo said, facing the direction of the Black Demon. "All of you."

"What about you?" Wade said.

"Yeah, Boss. We can't let you have all the fun."

"I need you back there and ready to high boost onto the beach when I tell you."

"But—"

"Go," Cujo shouted. "Now!"

"LARGE LIFEFORM DETECTED. WEST MOVING EAST. TWO HUNDRED FEET AND CLOSING."

"Already on our way to the beach, Pops," Maze said. "Benny forgot to mention that."

"Well excuse me for going for a more dramatic flare."

Cujo rolled his eyes, sighed and readied himself for the Black Demon.

The bloody waters churned in front of him. A few remaining body parts thumped against his suit. Smaller sharks darted away in every direction. They sensed something coming, no doubt. Something even they feared. Something old and menacing. An elder god returning from the depths to feast or breed once again...

For a second, he caught a glimpse of the monster. A massive black figure soon consumed in gore.

"Shit," Cujo said and glanced around.

His suit remained quiet. Blood throbbed along the side of his throat. A shiver held him for a second or two.

"Pops?" Maze said. "Everything good?"

He snorted. "Good? Uh, no. It's here, but there's so much blood...I can't tell where it went or if it moved at all."

"Why don't you just head our way?" Wade said. "Maybe if you run it'll chase you."

"Holy shit, the leprechaun is right," Benny said. "Basic predator instinct. Predators *want* their prey to run, right?"

"Sure," Cujo said, still looking for the Black Demon. "Don't run. Then what?"

"Um," Benny said. "Shoot it?"

Cujo sighed. "That doesn't help, jackass."

He scanned his surroundings for the monster, though found only swirling red water. An eyeball bobbed by his visor slow enough for him to make out the green iris. He was about to propel backwards in medium boost when it emerged from the watery horror show like the Devil himself. Black eyes like polished onyx gleamed. Its jaws opened and closed slowly, revealing its rows of jagged teeth.

All the strength leaked out of Cujo right then. He couldn't even open his mouth to command the suit. And the monster continued moving closer and closer. Its intent was clear. It wanted him to see it. It wanted him to be afraid. It wanted to make sure it was the last thing he saw before it chomped him to bits. Like it did with all the beach goers unlucky enough not to get out of the water in time. Dozens of gruesome deaths in only a few minutes.

Cujo was next.

The Black Demon knew who killed its mate. The six things in the ocean that shouldn't be in the ocean. It knew, and it wanted revenge. First it killed those people. Now it intended to kill the team.

Cujo swallowed and managed, "It's...it's here. It's looking right at me."

"LARGE LIFEFORM DETECTED," blared the suit, startling a gasp out of Cujo. "APPROACHING FROM THE WEST. EIGHTY FEET."

"Did I hear your suit right, Pops?" Maze said. "Eighty feet?"

"Yeah," he said, mind suddenly a blank slate.

Gone was any sense of a plan. Gone the will to move or fight. The ability to think evaporated the moment an idea formed. A slug. A mindless thing. Cujo floated in the blood-tinged waters and merely gaped at the monster glaring back at him. There was nothing more he could do. Fear gripped him in its skeletal claws and refused to let go.

"Boss?" Benny said.

"Pops? You there?"

He opened his mouth, but no words came out. Not a sound.

"I'll go check on him," Maze said.

"Me too," Wade said. "I'll back you up."

Cujo wanted to tell them no. Order them to standby. Anything. But he couldn't do it. This had never happened to him to such a degree before. Fear happened. Terror happened. Especially during a war and fighting monsters both human and nonhuman. But this...

"On our way, Pops," Maze said.

The Black Demon stopped moving and appeared to be just staring at Cujo now.

Cujo clenched his jaw and fought the terror gripping him. He needed to tell Maze and Wade to stay put.

"S-S..." He managed at first and tried again. "St—ay."

"What was that, Pops?"

"Stay," he said, focusing on the Black Demon. Anger eating away fear. Duty abolishing terror. "Stay where you are." It came out sounding like a plea, and in a way, it was. "Don't move until I say!"

"What?" Maze said. "You sure you're—"

"Return to your positions. Now."

Maze fell silent and Cujo continued to glare at the monster before him. This ancient thing. Spliced species. Supernatural. It didn't matter anymore. It had killed dozens of innocent people and before that, God knew how many hundreds, if not thousands. All because it wanted to. Not because it needed to. The intent was apparent, even to an old war dog like himself.

"Now," he shouted, finally finding his full voice.

"Okay, Pops," Maze said. "Don't have a stroke."

Cujo faced the Black Demon once more with not a blank mind, but one being consumed in gray battle fog. He knew exactly what was happening and had no control over it.

The Black Demon's jaws opened, and snapped shut. Body parts flailed in every direction.

"Come on, you bastard," Cujo said and drifted in the monster's direction. "Let's end this, motherfucker."

As if it heard him, the Black Demon charged.

Cujo blasted it with his AC-900, cutting its face into a hamburger with teeth.

Still, it surged forward, jaws widening.

Cujo roared, shifted his position and shot out one of its eyes.

And, still, it came.

Battle fog clearing a bit, he did the only choice his mind would cling to.

Cujo turned and high boosted toward the beach.

"Comin' in hot," he said.

"Standing by," Maze said.

"On the beach," Benny said. "Drinking margaritas and standing by. Am I right, Carl?"

Carl sighed through the speakers. Cujo concurred.

He didn't check to see if the monster was following him. No time. The ocean's floor already began to slope toward the surface. The beach would soon follow.

No time at all.

The bottom rose drastically and before Cujo could slow the suit down, he tumbled onto the beach and drove headfirst into the sand.

"Stop," he told the suit. It made a few clicking sounds and the boosters whirred to a stop.

He pushed himself out of the sand and rolled over onto his back. The sun glared through his visor. Too high in the sky. How long were they on the mission? A day? Two? Couldn't have been more than a day...

"Gotcha, Boss," Benny said and helped Cujo to his feet. "What happened to—"

"Holy *shit*," Maze shouted.

Cujo turned and all his blood froze as the massive shark barreled through the water and onto the beach like a hungry orca. Water and sand blasted the team, blinding Cujo before he could get his gun pointed at the monster. He moved backwards but had no idea if anything was behind him or not. If he tripped and fell, the Black Demon could snap him up.

"I got it," Carl said. "I—" A humph sound filled Cujo's helmet, then nothing but silence.

"Carl?" Benny said. "Fuck."

The sand dissipated, giving way to the beast itself, mutilated face and all. In its jaws, however, was one of the team. Didn't take long to figure out who. The crossbow-like weapon was enough. The Black Demon swayed back and forth, as though trying to crawl farther onto the beach to eat them all.

"It has Carl! Shoot out its teeth," Cujo said.

"I'm getting major pressure warnings," Carl shouted. "Starting to hurt!"

"Shoot its teeth," Cujo repeated and fired his AC-900 at the top teeth cutting into the chest of Carl's suit.

His team didn't miss a beat and gave the monster everything they had. The only teeth remaining were the smaller back rows. Carl plopped to the beach, and slowly crawled away.

"It's trying to get back into the water," Luna said.

The Black Demon wriggled back and forth and began sliding backwards. Back to the ocean. Back where it would heal and reemerge years later to toy with and kill more people.

They helped Carl up and Cujo said, "Kill it, Carl."

He swayed and through the speakers his breathing was heavy, but he lifted the powerful crossbow and pointed it at the Black Demon's head. He followed the back and forth motion of the giant shark's head.

"Come on, man," Benny said. "You got this. Just breathe."

"Kill it," Maze shouted.

"Shoot," Wade said.

"Now," Luna said.

A few seconds crawled by, and the Black Demon's bloody maw snapped. It was almost fully in the water now.

Carl straightened and said, "Goodnight."

A hole appeared in the monster's head, just above the nose and between the eyes. A hole which sizzled with green light. The cryptid shark's throes stopped. Its jaws quivered.

"Uh," Benny said. "Maybe we should all step back because—"

The Black Demon's head exploded in a burst of blood, brains, cartilage and flesh. All of it pummeled into the Cryptid Force Six. The blast itself was so strong it knocked them all onto their backs. Apparently, the suit's stabilizers didn't work as well out of the water.

Cujo closed his eyes and released a long breath. All the horror and terror eventually melted away, leaving him to stare at the bright blue sky above through bits and pieces of the Black Demon.

The Black Demon. A monster of legend...no more...

And although they searched, Mary was never found.

THIRTY-THREE

The Cryptid Force Six headquarters still stood, though in ruins.

"They took everything from the armory," Luna said and plopped down on a nearby chair. "Ammo. Even the prototypes."

"Kitchen is wiped out too," Wade said.

"No sign of Reece or Ross," Benny said as he sighed, and lowered his head.

"I found this on Reece's desk," Maze said and handed Cujo a small, black device.

He frowned and turned it over in his hands. "Looks like a hockey puck."

"I don't think Reece was a fan of hockey, though," Maze said.

Cujo nodded and noticed a slight impression along the side of the hockey puck-shaped device. Curious, he pressed the impression.

The puck vibrated in his hand, and he tossed it away. "Bomb!" He dove behind an overturned table.

When no explosion came, Benny said, "Uh, Boss. You need to look at this."

Cujo stood, glancing at the others. They were all looking at something and he followed their gaze.

On the floor was an almost life-sized hologram of Reece. She slowly looked around as if lost and said, "I don't know how much longer it will take for them to find me here." She glanced over her shoulder and looked back at the team, or whatever she was looking at during the time of the recording.

"Cujo, General Kyle and her team have infiltrated the headquarters. I set certain coordinates for the location one of the men said before I killed him. You'll find those taped to the bottom of my desk. They'll find me soon. I already hear them." She sighed and lowered her head. "I don't know where Ross is. Maybe they killed him. We got separated." She looked at the team, though Cujo felt like she was staring directly at him. "They might have cleaned out the armory. But there's an emergency one through a secret door at the back of the room. Left hook from the right." A crash sounded and Amanda Reece flickered out of existence.

The team stood there for a while, Cujo wasn't sure how long.

Finally, he straightened and said, "Okay. Let's find her." He turned toward Reece's desk when Maze grabbed his arm.

"Pops, it could be a trick."

He nodded, patted her hand and gently pulled out of her grip. "Could be." He walked to the desk, crouched and pulled a small notecard from the bottom.

"So," Maze said and crouched beside him. "You're just going to lead us to the slaughter? Is that it?"

Cujo stood and pocketed the notecard. "Nope. You all stay here. I might have cancer, but she needs help." He rushed out of Reece's office to the armory.

At a pegboard, he found the third hook from the right and pulled it. Nothing happened. He wiggled it. Nothing happened.

"It's made to hold guns, Boss," Benny said and pushed the hook upward.

Something gave a muffled beep. A click followed. Then the wall hissed and swung slowly open.

Cujo grunted. "Thanks."

He descended a few steps into another armory, albeit a bit smaller than the main one. It took him a bit, but he found the ammo cans for his AC-900. He grabbed two and turned to leave.

"You'll probably need more than that," Luna said. "I'll get you another one."

"Thanks," he said and stepped by Wade and Benny to the main armory.

He found a wheeled cart and placed the ammo cans, which held approximately twelve hundred rounds. Luna slammed a third can on the cart and smiled. Cujo smiled back and turned to get one more can, ammo for his pistol, a claymore or two and some grenades. Wade hefted two more cans of ammo and walked by Cujo to the cart.

Cujo stopped and glanced at his team, who gathered around him. He sighed and flapped his arms in something like exasperation, though not quite.

"Thanks for the help. I just...Reece needs me. Her dad was a good man and without her, there wouldn't be a Cryptid Force Six. Her knowledge..." He trailed off, trying not to get too emotional.

Eventually, he continued. "Her knowledge of cryptids. Her desire to help and save lives. As far as I'm concerned, she's family. I'm not going to stop until I find her."

Cujo moved toward the secret armory.

"Where you go," Benny said, "we go, Boss."

He stopped and turned back to his team. His family. They stood at attention; Carl included. Cujo waved a dismissive hand. "Stop that. At ease."

They relaxed and Maze said, "We're with you. She's important to us too."

"Same," Luna said.

"Oorah," Wade said.

Carl glanced at everyone, shrugged and looked Cujo in the eyes. "I'm in, if you'll have me."

Cujo grunted and turned back to the secret armory. "Lock and load."

THE END

SEVEREDPRESS

CHECK OUT OTHER GREAT BIGFOOT NOVELS

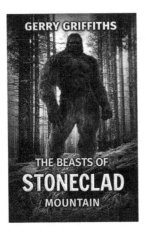

THE BEASTS OF STONECLAD MOUNTAIN
by Gerry Griffiths

Clay Morgan is overjoyed when he is offered a place to live in a remote wilderness at the base of a notorious mountain. Locals say there are Bigfoot living high up in the dense mountainous forest. Clay is skeptic at first and thinks it's nothing more than tall tales.

But soon Clay becomes a believer when giant creatures invade his new home and snatch his baby boy, Casey.

Now, Clay and his wife, Mia, must rescue their son with the help of Clay's uncle and his dog, a journey up the foreboding mountain that will take them into an unimaginable world...straight into hell!

BIGFOOT AWAKENED
by Alex Laybourne

A weekend away with friends was supposed to be fun. One last chance for Jamie to blow off some steam before she leaves for college, but when the group make a wrong turn, fun is the last thing they find.

From the moment they pass through a small rural town they are being hunted by whatever abominations live in the woods.

Yet, as the beasts attack and the truth is revealed, they learn that despite everything, man still remains the most terrifying evil of them all.

CHECK OUT OTHER GREAT CRYPTID NOVELS

RETURN TO DYATLOV PASS
by J.H. Moncrieff

In 1959, nine Russian students set off on a skiing expedition in the Ural Mountains. Their mutilated bodies were discovered weeks later. Their bizarre and unexplained deaths are one of the most enduring true mysteries of our time. Nearly sixty years later, podcast host Nat McPherson ventures into the same mountains with her team, determined to finally solve the mystery of the Dyatlov Pass incident. Her plans are thwarted on the first night, when two trackers from her group are brutally slaughtered. The team's guide, a superstitious man from a neighboring village, blames the killings on yetis, but no one believes him. As members of Nat's team die one by one, she must figure out if there's a murderer in their midst—or something even worse—before history repeats itself and her group becomes another casualty of the infamous Dead Mountain.

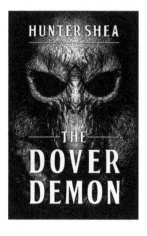

DOVER DEMON
by Hunter Shea

The Dover Demon is real...and it has returned. In 1977, Sam Brogna and his friends came upon a terrifying, alien creature on a deserted country road. What they witnessed was so bizarre, so chilling, they swore their silence. But their lives were changed forever. Decades later, the town of Dover has been hit by a massive blizzard. Sam's son, Nicky, is drawn to search for the infamous cryptid, only to disappear into the bowels of a secret underground lair. The Dover Demon is far deadlier than anyone could have believed. And there are many of them. Can Sam and his reunited friends rescue Nicky and battle a race of creatures so powerful, so sinister, that history itself has been shaped by their secretive presence?

CHECK OUT OTHER GREAT CRYPTID NOVELS

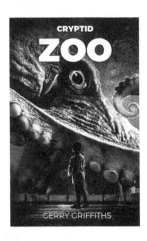

Made in United States
North Haven, CT
19 May 2022

19355168R00088